LOST SOWLS

R J SMITH

Scottish Workshop Publications

British Library Cataloguing in Publication Data

ISBN 978-1-873577-53-0

Copyright © Scottish Workshop Publications 2009

Robert J Smith retains the right to be acknowledged sole author and confirms that all characters, apart from those in the public domain, are fictional and that any resemblance to living persons is purely coincidental.

No part of this book may be reproduced by any means or transmitted or translated into a language or machine language or stored in a retrieval system without formal written permission of Scottish Workshop Publications. Permission is normally available without charge for reproductions clearly intended to benefit Deaf people or their organizations.

Requests for sales information, review copies and notice of further Publication should be addressed to SWP/SCVO, Traquair Centre, 15 Mansfield Place, Edinburgh, EH3 6BB, Scotland.

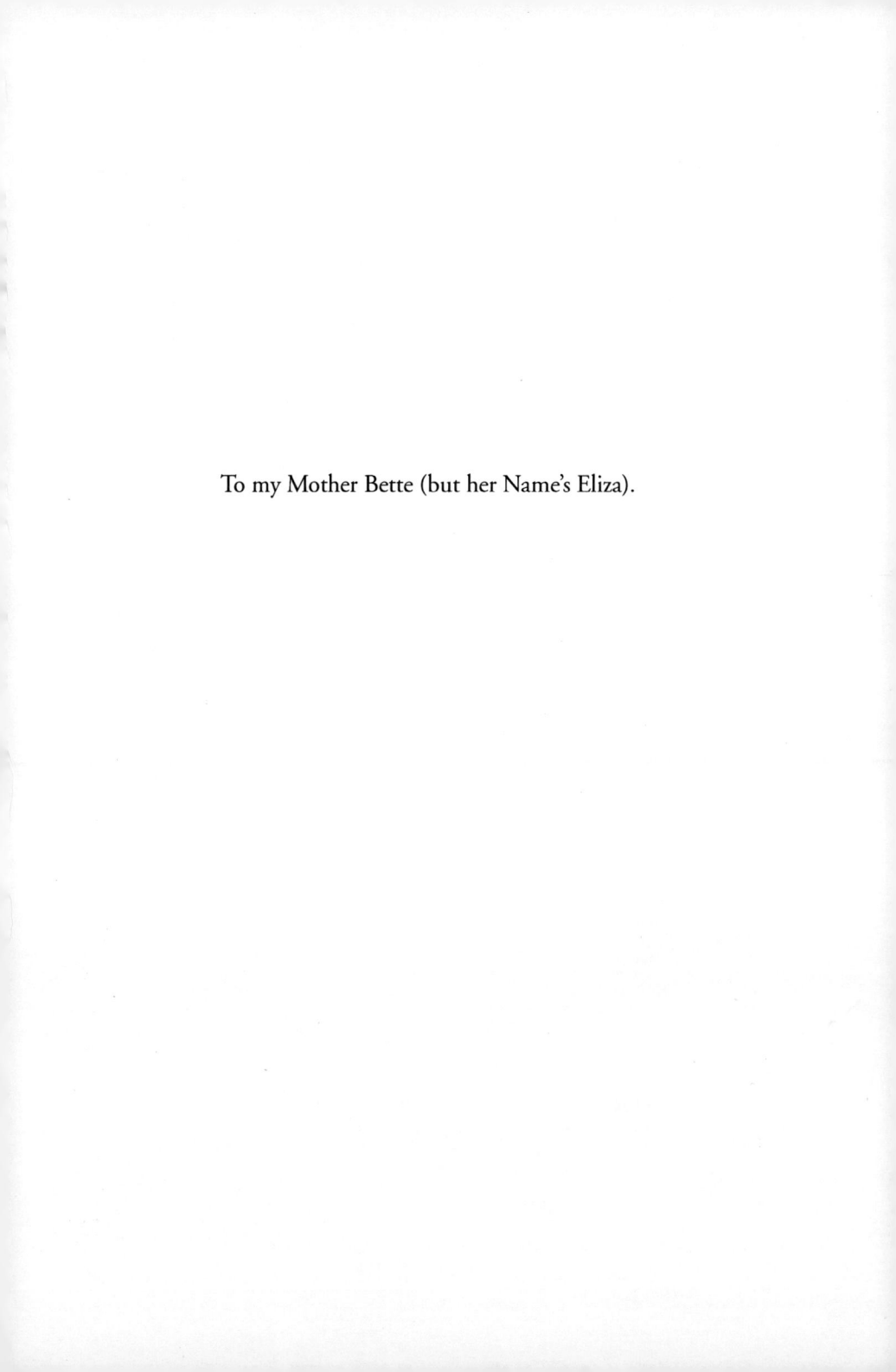

To my Mother Bette (but her Name's Eliza).

ACKNOWLEDGEMENTS

Thanks to Rowan and Lewis for their encouragement and 'technical support'. To my Mother for her patience with my endless questions on Wishaw in the Thirties. To the hugely talented Kirsty Macrae for her superb cover artwork. To George Montgomery, as ever, for his editing and perceptive comments. To Joan Montgomery for her panache and literary lunches. Last but not least to my wife Joanne for her unceasing faith that this fictional foray into psychic archaeology would see the light of day.

Prologue

'Mony a yin for him maks mane,
But nane sall ken whaur he has gane,
Ower his white banes as they grow bare,
The Wind sall blaw for Evermair.'

(The Twa Corbies)

In March 1932 Gerard Rolink of the Benhar Moss Litter Co was digging peat on Greenhead Moss near Cambusnethan, Wishaw, when his spade struck wood a short distance below the surface. On widening his excavation, Rolink found five pieces of birchwood, and below them the fully clothed body of a man. Little remained of the body, save for the upper part of the skull, both femurs and some teeth. The clothes, however, were in a remarkable state of preservation. Part of the skull, and some hair six inches long had been preserved beneath a woollen cap. The man was dressed in a high quality woollen jacket, short leather breeches, long woollen stockings and well-made pointed leather shoes, with the buckles missing.

Mr Rolink, no doubt in a state of some agitation, set off quickly to Newmains Police Station, and returned with Superintendent Aitken of Bellshill Police. The remains were sketched and carefully removed to the Police Station, all relics being retained in the original position. It was clear that the body was of considerable antiquity. The Procurator Fiscal, James Adair, on being informed of the situation, telephoned the Archaeologist Ludovic McLellan Mann, who subsequently made a detailed examination of the remains with the aid of various specialists.

Analysis of the jacket revealed that it had been made around the period 1680-1690; a turbulent period of history in this area of Scotland - sometimes known as 'The Killing Times'. Covenanter Forces had defeated the Royalists at Drumclog in 1679, before they themselves were routed at Bothwell Bridge. Troops of Royalist dragoons and foot soldiers roamed the countryside in the aftermath and in subsequent years, hunting down those still faithful to the Covenant.

The dental remains indicated that the man was around 50 years old, backed up by the fact that his hair was greying. The femurs indicated that the man was of moderate height, around 5' 6".

The cap, where it covered the back of the neck, had a sharp cut, as had the front of the right shoe, both in the sole and the upper. These were probably as a result of sword thrusts, and would have caused serious, perhaps fatal wounds. The left femur was broken.

The body seems to have been buried without ceremony in this shallow grave, the excavation of which would only have taken a short time. The five pieces of birch wood seem to have been placed with some care over the body. Perhaps, as Mann suggests in his report, they were used as an improvised stretcher, in which case four people would have been required to transport the body. However, the care with which they were placed may suggest that in accordance with old superstition they were laid over the body to stop the ghost from walking.

As Mann writes: " The place is at the centre of a large stretch of peat and marsh, treeless and without dwellings. Deep open drains, well filled with water, cut across the moor in various directions. A century or two ago the area must have been wetter and less accessible." Clearly some pains were taken to dispose of the body in a clandestine manner. Therefore by far the strongest possibility, due to the evidence of violence and other factors, is that the man was murdered and the body concealed to keep the deed secret. Given the dating evidence it may well be that his violent death was connected to the current religious disturbances.

Who was he? The quality of the clothing suggests that the victim did not belong to the lowest level of society. It is unclear whether he was a soldier or civilian. If he was a Royalist soldier, then he was a foot soldier or militiaman. Dragoons would have worn boots.

It is recorded that several Covenanters were cut down and killed by marauding Royalist forces in the region. It is unlikely if this were the case that the Royalists would have taken the trouble to bury him. If Covenanting friends had located the body, he would have been buried as a martyr in consecrated ground.

Perhaps he was a Royalist sympathiser or agent, passing on information to those seeking to hunt down Covenanters, or perhaps just some unfortunate soul who simply met with misadventure.

The mystery of the Cambusnethan murder remains.

NOTES

The novel is set in the days preceding the discovery of the body, and at the time of the deed itself. It explores a possible, but not necessary likely, murder scenario, as well as the events and personalities surrounding the discovery. Dialogue, where appropriate, is in a toned down version of the local vernacular, as to have characters in 1930s Lanarkshire, far less characters in the Lanarkshire of the 1680s, speak in Standard English seems at the very least inauthentic. Some characters are loosely based on real people. Sadly, or perhaps fortunately, the Wutchstane is entirely a figment of my imagination. The body was discovered on 23rd March 1932, but I took the small liberty of placing it at the Vernal Equinox, a little earlier. It should also be noted that most 'alignments' on Megalithic sites, tend to correspond to sunrise and sunset at the Solstices rather than the Equinoxes.

The Archaeologist's Report on the discovery can be found in the 'Transactions of the Glasgow Archaeological Society', Volume 9, Part 1. An account of the work of the colourful and controversial archaeologist Ludovic McLellan Mann can be found in the 'Proceedings of the Society of Antiquaries of Scotland', Vol. 132 (2002). A memorial to the Covenanting preacher Donald Cargill is located near Covington, under the flanks of Tinto Hill, close to where he was betrayed and captured at Covington Mill.

A plaque to the memory of the murdered man, headed to 'The Unknown Soldier' (assuming he was a soldier) was erected on Greenhead Moss, close to where his body was found. As for his remains, they were deposited in Kelvingrove Museum, Glasgow, where they lie to this day.

CHAPTER 1

<u>March 1932</u>
Suddenly, the bright shafts of other worldly daylight in Tommy's skull faded. There was a black cape of darkness only.
Then softly the blue mutter of dawn crept into the sleeping room, caressing his leaden eyelids. Outside there was the fierce whoosh of an express on the South line, and the moan of a work's siren.
He awoke with a start. A dark suited figure by the bedside glowered down at him. Tommy turned away and hid under the bedclothes, neck prickling at the certainty of iron fingers round his throat.
"Naw, this isnae happenin, Ah'm still dreamin!" he told himself after a moment's quivering tension.
Determinedly, he jerked himself round and faced his nightmare. Auld Ridnose, the Heidie, remained, scowling metallically. He thrust forward his arm and waggled his finger, his mouth framing the word 'C'mere', but no words came.
Tommy shuddered and shook free of the reality of the waking nightmare. The Headmaster blinked out of existence.
Tommy stared at the wall; awake at last.
"Ah'm no gaun tae school!" he ground out, "away an pee yersel Ridnose!"
That was it. He luxuriated in the soft wash of freedom that his decision bestowed on him. The day now had infinite possibilities. His head filled with the dream light once more as the dark corridors of Conformity were banished into the realms of Tomorrow.
Heavy hoofbeats and the rumble of the milk cart in the street outside called him back to practical matters.
Clenching his teeth, he rolled out of bed.
Prepared as he was for the chill of the room, he was not prepared enough. The raw cold came at him with a rush. He held his body hard against it, refusing to shiver. He clutched his jersey and breeks, and had them on in seconds. Only then did he allow himself the luxury of a prolonged shiver.
He shambled over to the ewer, noting idly the intricate network of spiders'

web cracks which radiated darkly over the glaze as he gave himself a Cat's Lick with the last trickle of the ice cold water left in the jug from the previous day. As his fingers pierced the surface, he imagined he could feel a hard crust of ice on the water.

After wiping his hands on his sleeve, he hacked a doorstep of staley loaf and spread it with a thin layer of margarine. As he gobbled his breakfast, he stuck his head round the door of the other room.

Big Geordie, his Stepfather, mouth gaping open, hung precariously on the edge of the Hole in the Wa' bed. Obviously still in a drunken stupor, he grunted like a pig wallowing in the sharn. The fat bastard!

Last night he'd come in roaring fou; he'd near kicked the door in.

He'd won two quid at Pitch and Toss and had drunk it away in Girdwood's within a few hours.

Tommy had cowered in his bed as his mother had screamed abuse. She'd been with Geordie for the first hour or so of his spree, but had stalked off when he started to become argumentative.

So when he breinged in at near half eleven there was Hell to pay. As usual the tirade ended when Geordie, by then too dulled to answer her back, walloped her and sent her sprawling across the room. Tommy had peeked fearfully out of the curtain which screened his bed from the rest of the room. His mother lay sobbing in a crumpled heap whilst Geordie lurched over to the open door and peed at the stars.

There had come a battery of knocks from the ceiling as Tam Chalmers chapped down from the house above. Geordie glowered up but said nothing. He staggered over to his wife and courssly picked her up.

" 'Moan Hen," he said in an approximation of tenderness and hauled her off to bed.

Now Tommy looked at the sleeping figure of his mother as she huddled into this great brute of a man. The black rose of a bruise starred her forehead. Another wave of anger, partly directed at his own impotence, swept over him.

"Ye piggin bastard, wan o these days ah'm gaun tae thrapple ye while ye're sleepin. Ah could dae it the noo!"

His knuckles whitened at the thought: he could hear the gurgles in Geordie's throat as he worried the life out of him with the iron collar of his bare hands. He imagined Geordie's blue skin and dead fish eyes as they laid his bloated corpse, mouth agape, on a cold, white slab.

Tommy turned away. What made him think like this? He was contemplating murder. Folk weren't allowed to do that. Anyway they'd hing him if he did. Big Geordie must be on Afternoon Shift; if he wasn't he'd be getting the sack. That was one thing he was careful about: he was always out in time for his shift down at the Stenton Steelworks. Jobs were hard to come by, as you could see from the gloomy knots of the workless at every corner of Wishie Main Street at all hours of the day.

Geordie, though a boozer, considered himself above the unemployed. "Ma faither's faither wis gentry ye ken!" was his boast to all and sundry. He wasn't so daft as to lose his job through latecoming.

"Time ah wis awa," thought Tommy.

He turned into the front room, picked up his boots, and studied the greasy face of the clock on the mantelpiece as he laced them up.

"Aye, this would be a guid time tae leave the hoose," he thought. " Ah kin be weel oot o this area afore anybody's settin oot tae Beltanfit."

He tutted in irritation as one of the lengths of string which served as his laces snapped. He hurled the snapped off length in the general direction of the grate and tied a knot only half way up the tongue of the well scuffed, tacketty boots. His big toes protruded through the burst seams at the front, but since the boots had long since ceased to fit him, this made for a measure of comfort if not protection from the elements.

Without a backward glance, he quietly let himself out through he front door, gasping as his lungs caught the frosty March air. He noted that even the wall which separated Smith's Land from Miller Street was well dusted by rime. Yesterday's dubs in the bare earth path that led to the close through to Hill Street were opaque pools of creeping ice. He brought down his heel on one. Water seeped brownly as the impact fractures rippled along the surface of the icy mirror.

A train cleared its throat, then huffed out of the nearby Central Station as he exited the close into Hill Street. He headed past Girdwood's in the direction of the Station Steps, since that was the way he generally went to school.

He crossed the street and peered in the window of Ikey Moses' shop and eyed avidly the clamjamphrie of colour in the window: jars of Stripit Balls, Hogey Pogey Eyes, Soor Plooms and Sherbet Dabs. As ever, he hadn't even a farthing in his breiks pocket. His eyes caught the slim figure of Ikey Moses himself gazing out at him with a careworn expression. Tommy waved jauntily in, but Ikey stared straight through him, clearly oblivious of his

3

presence. Tommy shrugged his shoulders and strode past the Coalry to the Station Steps.

At the top he halted. This was his eyrie. From here he fondly imagined that he could see half of Scotland. To the north was the long grey blue line of the Campsies, hard edged against the fug and stour of Glasgow and Motherwell. Behind him, to the east, Hill Street climbed up to Wishie Main Street, where the Toon Knock soared above a sea of bare trees ahint.

But it was the south and west that mainly attracted his gaze. Here lay the great fold of the Clyde Valley, its far rim propping up the sky. He loved to study its changing moods; the vast game of Shadow chasing Light, and Light chasing Shadow as the clouds' silhouettes stealthily scaled its flanks. He spotted the changes in its tapestry as they happened : the first turning of the trees or their first blooming, the ripening of the grain or the first ploughing. These things represented the changing rhythms of the year.

Today the furrows of the High Parks were fingered with last week's snow, as if a titanic hyperborean beast had attempted to claw down the earth to bare rock. A vague, grey line of mist dogged the lower horizon where the valley plunged to the fertile haughs and the forever hidden Clyde. He imagined the dank chill of the Valley floor in contrast to the glinting cold clarity of the High Parks.

He shivered uncontrollably and tucked his tattered jersey into his breiks. His only jacket was several sizes too small for him and he'd long since ceased to wear it. He eyed the lift appraisingly. There was hardly a cloud to be seen. "It'll soon warm up," he muttered aloud.

As his mind reverted to the practical matters of the day, he gazed idly down the flight of steps leading to the platform of the Central Station. It was almost deserted, save for two smartly dressed young women, who huddled in a corner giggling furtively, and a bowler hatted gent who stalked irritably up and down the platform, obviously annoyed that he'd missed the previous train to Glasgow.

Tommy took a few steps down the great flight leading to Station Road. Beyond the reek from the Stenton Raws, Beltanfit School was deserted. Not even the Heidie would be in yet.

He wavered for a moment. It would be a lot easier for him to go than to plunk it. Save for the Heidie, it was not the maisters or the schoolwork he feared: he was a bright lad and the learning came easily to him. He dreaded the jibes and resentment of his classmates. Many of them could not abide the fact that someone who was so poor as to be dressed like a tattie bogle should be one of the brightest pupils in the school. This, in their eyes, was against the natural order of things. Surely academic ability was wasted on such a tink. It was not as if his main tormentors were much better off or much better dressed than he; far from it. He was an oddity, and they acted much as a flock of birds who would ruthlessly attack a deformed or aberrantly plumaged individual. He scanned the High Parks regretfully. Somewhere in a farm above Rigside his best chum Rab McKay was working a term as a halflin. Rab had left Beltanfit at Christmas. His wee sister Betty had told him last week that Rab hated it; the Grieve was gey sore on him. She'd said that he'd confided in her on her last visit that he was thinking of running away. If only Rab were here now.

The contrast between the bright patchwork of the Parks and the squat drabness of Beltanfit decided him. He knew that they'd send out the Attendance Officer and that he'd catch it, but that was in the future and it wouldn't be the first time.

He gingerly negotiated his way down the glistening steps and turned left past the Stables into Caley Road.

The question of how to spend his day of freedom was beyond doubt. He'd head for Greenhead Moss. The Moss was a great expanse of peat and marshy wilderness to the east of Wishie, lying between Camnethan and Waterloo. It held a great fascination for Tommy who always returned sooner or later.

Now, anxious to avoid being spotted and inevitably clyped on by any of his classmates, he scurried along the backstreets, avoiding a route by the main roads.

The plan seemed to have worked, since by the time he reached the end of Stewarton Street, he had encountered nothing but the normal morning bustle of workers and shopkeepers opening for daily business. But as he passed the last tenement block a rough cry sounded at his heels.

"Haw!"

A big sandy haired heifer of a lad leaned against the close mouth of the tenement. Tommy grimaced. Big Carrot Heid, one of his chief oppressors at school.

"Whit d'ye want?" Tommy stared hard at him, irritation turning into hardly veiled aggression.

"Ye no gaun tae schule the day?"

"Aye, ah'm gaun!"

"Whit are ye daein up here well? Whaur are ye gaun tae?"

"Ah'm gaun a message fur ma Mother, no that it's any o your business!" Carrot Heid drew him a look of extreme disbelief.

"Naw ye're no, ah think ye're pluggin it. Ah'm gaun tae tell on ye, Smelly Nellie!"

"Dae whit ye like," snapped Tommy, turning on his heels, "but ye're wrang, ah'm daein a message!"

"Are ye pickin up some money for yer Maw, or is she sendin ye oot for a man: everybody kens she's a hoor!" chortled Carrot Heid, repeating some of the local gossip.

Tommy seized a half brick lying by the roadside, whirled round and hurled it with all his force at the lie. Carrot Heid duked into the close and the brick spattered harmlessly at the close mouth.

Tommy charged, steaming with fury, into the close. Carrot Heid's hurried footfalls echoed on the upper landing.

"Ah'll get ye for this! Come doon here an gie me a square go ye muckle keech!" yelled Tommy.

A slammed door upstairs announced that Carrot Heid was not keen to take up the challenge. Frustrated, Tommy kicked out at a fragment of the brick he'd thrown, then rushed out of the close and trotted off in the direction of the Moss, hoping that distance would wipe out this unpleasant incident. But the insult to his Mother still burned.

It was true that she'd gone off the rails after his father had been killed near the end of the War. He hadn't even been born then. His Father had never seen him. The only mementoes of his Father that remained were a few faded photographs, which lay deep in the top drawer of the sideboard, his gold ring, which he'd been promised when he reached the age of sixteen, and his encyclopaedias.

After his birth they'd lived through the grey days with his Grandfather and Grandmother in their cramped room and kitchen. His paternal Grandparents had bitterly disapproved of their son's marriage and disowned Tommy and his Mother; and, as if to reinforce the fact, they had moved out of the area, broken hearted at their only son's death.

Then at the end of 1920, his Gran had died of the flu.

This had been the final straw for Agnes his mother. Though she had taken to drink before, she now started drinking with whatever company she could find. She'd become involved in a number of street fights, had appeared in front of the Bailies at the Court, and had been fined on several occasions. Naturally this had given her a bad reputation. She'd been christened 'Black Aggie' by the local children, who would cry it after her as she stalked the streets fou as a puggie.

In those days as now, Tommy had been left to fend mostly for himself. When sober, his mother would make some token attempt at caring for him, but these occasions were few and far between. His Grandfather, courss as he was, had given more love and attention than ever his mother had done. Tommy remembered overhearing a furious altercation between his Mother and his Grandfather a few years back, just before his Grandfather had died. After it had emerged that Agnes had drunk away most of her pay, his Granda had angrily retorted:-

"Ye limmer, ye dinnae care tuppence aboot yon puir boy o yours. His claes are aw threidbare, an ye spend aw yer pey on drink! Ah havenae the money tae buy claes for him the noo!"

"Ah didnae ask tae have him!" Agnes had snapped back in return.

"Naw, ye dinnae care aboot yer man either, him that died in the War for ye!"

"Ah only marriet him because ah had tae, ye mind how ye made me dae it."

"Ah didnae want folk tae think ye were a hoor. Ye were gey lucky that boy wantit tae mairry ye. His folks didnae want him tae. He wis a fine boy, better than ye deserved for sure!"

At that point, practical matters had intruded.

"Aye, an whit aboot ma rent money? Have ye drunk that awa tae?"

"Naw, ah put it ahint the clock," she'd replied coolly.

That summed up the contradictions in his Mother. Even during the worst of her drinking, she'd held down a job; first in the Battleaxe Works, then in King's Sweetie Works. She always kept herself spick and span. Whatever her state the night before, she'd be out of the house, face freshly rouged and dressed in her neat cross over blue uniform, in plenty of time for the day's shift.

She never brought drink into the house, even if it meant drinking up a close from a bottle of Eldorado. But she'd always said that she could handle the drink; it wasn't her master. To be sure, even when apparently in a stupor, always those eyes stared out at you like clear pools and there was always a cool tongue in her head.

As regards rent she'd always paid her way. She certainly faced her financial, if not parental responsibilities.

Then, just as her Father was dying, she'd taken up with Geordie Brawley, and a few months after Granda's death, she'd given up her job and moved in with him as a Common Law Wife. The following year they were married.
Her drinking had eased dramatically then. Occasionally she went through the motions to keep her man company. But it was clear that she didn't give two hoots about the drink now. Erstwhile drinking cronies remembered her boast.
Tommy snapped out of his reverie and eyed a team of Clydesdales, a grey vaporous veil hovering above them in the crisp air as their dray was unloaded at Barr's Ginger works at the corner of Greenhead Road. Suddenly his problems were behind him; the Moss and the lands of Greenhead lay before him.
A surge of joy enveloped him as he cast off his mantle of daily cares. With a gallus stride he linked up the hill, the soles of his feet skittering and sliding beneath him on the hoary grass.
In spite of his blythe demeanour, he made a point of avoiding the Auld Shafts. The ground was crumbly and liable to subside. Folk said that two boys had fallen down one of the shafts a few years back. Late on an Autumn night it had been, and there had been no one in the vicinity to hear their yellochs. They'd been found the next day frozen to death: or the way some others told it, they were frichtent to death by the spirits of the lang deid miners, men and boys, that lay buried underground, their bodies ne'er recovered from the shafts.
Whatever the truth of the matter, Tommy gave the area a wide berth.
His initial destination was the Perchie Pond. He reckoned that this morning it might be possible to skate.
At the crest of the hill, he halted and scanned the valley. The thin layer of mist had evaporated, and the parks flashed malachite and ochre in the creeping sunlight. To the south Tinto, snow shouldered, was the mighty sentinel of the Southern Uplands.
This familiar landscape, so often viewed in a momentary pause on his way to school, and so often representing unattainable freedom, was now his to drink in at his leisure. He had all day to do so.
A peezer careened above him, tumbling in its daft Spring display flight. Peewit! Peewit! Tommy grinned. They'd be nesting soon.
He turned and cut a swathe through the stiff grass, following the line of the Wee Plantation towards the Perchie.

There it lay, surface hard with blue white ice. By the rushes a few dark pools of water steamed. He heard the craik of a water hen, banished to this small refuge. Observing the pools, he doubted whether the ice would be thick enough to support his weight. He had learned to be a canny laddie, not given to taking unnecessary risks. Retaining one foot on firm ground, he placed the other gingerly on the ice, keeping his weight on the rear foot. It seemed firm enough. He shifted his centre of balance forward onto the leading foot. The ice still seemed rock solid. He launched his other foot forward. Immediately there was an alarming report as the ice protested at the weight. Without hesitation, Tommy birled round and louped towards dry land.

Slightly annoyed, though not surprised, he prised a frost fused chuckie from the ground and launched it at the ice. It bounced and skidded along the surface as if it had suddenly gained a deranged life of its own. He kent fine that he'd been a gowk to expect skateable ice in March.

He snapped a reed and stalked the margin of the Perchie. A grey mound protruding through the surface caught his attention. At first glance it loked like an old coat, but it seemed too sleek for that. With the heel of his boot, he crashed through the ice surrounding the object. Immediately a foul reek of rotting flesh leapt at him. Bubbles of putrifaction danced to the surface with oily pops. It was a body! Tommy felt the boak rise in his throat. He turned away and staggered off to breathe in the clean air, the iron hammers of fear and shock pounding inside.

What was he going to do? Someone had been murdered. The bloated visage of a corpse, oddly like Geordie Brawley, smirked at him momentarily. Then common sense reasserted itself. Aye, it was a body, but he hadn't had a good look at it, so it could be the body of anything. Determinedly he retraced his steps. At the tip of the sleek body, a long jawed skull, thinly stretched with flesh and with prominent canine teeth, yawed gently in the small pool.

"It's a dug!" he exclaimed aloud in relief. "Puir thing, some bugger's droont it. Imagine me thinkin it wis somebody!"

Tommy didn't tarry however. He strode off, affecting an air of braggadocio to cover the fright he'd had. He decided to head for the Moss Coup. There were aye good pickings there he reminded himself.

The Coup lay by the auld railway, not far from Camnethan Cemetery. He progressed down the line of the abandoned track which had served some of the disused mines in the area.

The frost was lifting now; the taller tufts of grass were turning green as they lost their white sheen. Tommy stamped his feet and jumped on the spot to get the feeling back into his toes. The insides of his boots squelched with icy water, so that he progressed with a weird lurching gait.

He always spent a lot of time at the various coups in the area. The Moss Coup was one of the best. The Caley Coup was more extensive, but there were more quality finds to be had at the Moss Coup since Camnethan had more early settlement than Wishaw or Wishawtoun as it was formerly called. Grubbing about coups was more than a game to him; it was a Quest. He saw himself as an eminent archaeologist engaged in excavating a forgotten Tell in a desert landscape which had formerly been a centre of a fabulous lost race in the halcyon days of Civilisation.

His interest had been stirred by a few brief paragraphs in his most precious possession: his eight volumes of the 'Modern Cyclopaedia'. These had belonged to his Father, and he kept them lovingly wrapped in newspaper below his bed.

He'd written of his interest in a school essay. His English teacher, Miss Campbell, who had always seemed extremely sympathetic towards him, had started loaning him books on the subject. He learned of the work of the great pioneers of Archaeology- Schliemann, Botta, Layard, Rawlinson, Dorpfeld, Petrie and Evans. He'd marvelled at the wondrous discoveries of Wooley and Carter. These visions sustained him through the swarms of playground taunts and minor persecutions.

He had arranged his discoveries: clay pipe bowls and stems, glass bools from old Codd ginger bottles and fragments of old crockery (labelled 'potsherds'), in meticulous order inside old shoe boxes, which he kept by his encyclopaedias.

Though rummaging about coups was by no means an uncommon occurrence, his contemporaries called him 'The Coupie', 'Neillie the Tink', or most commonly, 'Smelly Nellie', no doubt being influenced by his generally neglected and poor-house appearance.

The Coup was screened from his view by an arm of Greenhead Plantation, but when it came into view as he rounded a bend in the auld track, he tutted in dismay.

There was a wee cluster of folk at the Coup, heads bent as they scanned the surface.

Tommy's pace slowed, but as the track snaked nearer, a great fusillade of

barking erupted. A lean tyke bounded towards him from the Coup.
Tommy stood stock still as it approached, red eyed and slevering. It stalked right up to him, not pausing to bowf a short distance away as dogs often do. It had a wild and gallus air. It gurled deeply, then sniffed at his crotch and dreeped great muckle gobs of slever down his legs. Tommy broke out into a cold sweat, encountering for the first time one of the most primeval of male fears; that of imminent castration.
Just as the first thoughts of some desperate action began to slink into his consciousness, a shrill two tone whistle echoed near at hand. The dog pricked up its ears and darted off at high speed without a backward glance towards a small boy who had appeared close by. The boy cuffed the dog, which lay down, crestfallen. He strode over to Tommy, who stood transfixed.
Tommy could see at a glance that this was a Tinker laddie. Though he looked only about nine or ten, he held himself with a hard, confident air. He was totty, lean and wiry; not a pick on him. His breiks and jersey were in tatters, making Tommy's own garb seem positively well to do. His face and legs were caked with deep-seated grime, and waves of the minging stink of unwashed flesh almost turned Tommy's stomach.
But from that manky face, fremmit, dark eyes flared like twin embers.
"Whaur div ye think ye're gaun?" he demanded.
"Ah wis gaun tae the Coup," Tommy replied truthfully.
"Weel ye canna, yon Coup's oors!"
He spoke in a lilting tone, obviously not local, which to Tommy's ears, somewhat negated the boy's anger.
Growing more confident, Tommy glared down at the lad, realising that he was fully a head smaller than himself.
"It's no anybody's coup. Ah've been howkin there for fower years an ah've never seen ye afore, sae how can it be yours?"
"The Gamey seyed it wis oors tae howk as we like, as lang as we gie him a share o whitever we find."
"The Gamey? Whit, 'Buck' Rogers?" snorted Tommy, "he's bummin his load. He's got naethin tae dae wi the Coup, he juist owns the shootin rights for the Moss, he's tryin tae do ye!"
"Whit?" The boy scratched his shaggy mane of hair. "Come wi me ower til ma faither an tell him aa whit ye've juist tellt me."
"Aye, aw richt," replied Tommy, rather amused at exposing the deception that the gamey had tried to perpetrate on these folk.

The Tinker family: a man, woman and three bairns, gathered round as Tommy repeated his statement to the father, a dark, shilpit man in a decrepit jacket and tweed bunnet. The Tink grinned slowly. "D'ye trew that ah'd let on if we airt oot anythin guid; if he'd speired ah'd hae seyed naethin. Anywey ah thank ye laddie."

"It's nae bother Mister. Yon auld whitterick thinks he owns everythin between Camnethan an Waterloo, he's aye chasin me. Whit are ye lookin for in the Coup anywey?"

"We're leukin fur scrap metal, banes, rags, onythin at aa' but there's nae ower much tae be had here ah jaloose."

"Ah could hae tellt ye that, as ah've juist tellt your boay, ah've been howkin here for fower years."

"Oh aye, an whit are ye leukin fur?"

"Auld bottle or gless, cley pipes or challogies, bits o chinny an aw that."

"Bi Christ laddie," a look of incredulity stole over the Tink's face, "ah thocht it wia me that gethert the trasherie. Whit div ye want wi aa thon?"

"Och, ye widnae unnerstaun!" declared Tommy with a faint grin.

CHAPTER 2

After spending several hours with the Tinkers on the Coup, Tommy tired of excavation. Within the first half hour, he'd discovered a cache of clay pipe stems and heads, a clay doll and some clay marbles.
He'd muttered aloud in wonder," The treasure o Priam!"
On hearing this, the Tinker woman and the eldest girl had exchanged meaningful glances which clearly indicated that the laddie was wannert.
Since then he'd found nothing save the occasional fragment of blue and white china. Still, he was more than satisfied with the morning's work.
"Ah'm awa ower the Moss noo, ah'll see ye again." He announced his departure.
"Aye, ye ken whaur we'll be. Either that or ower by Waterloo whaur we're bidin."
The father stretched himself and yawned, then studied Tommy intently for the first time.
"Div ye no gae til the Schule laddie?"
"No the day anyway," smirked Tommy.
"Ye'll catch it frae the Dominie!"
Tommy shrugged his shoothers in bravado. Eyeing the boy he asked, "Whit aboot yer ain boay an yer lassies?"
"We hae nae need fur schules or dominies. We hae oor ain weys," interjected the boy with quiet pride.
Tommy nodded, and set off without a backward glance.
As he rounded the edge of the Plantation, a whaup soared overhead, its call of lonely muirs and shivery desolation filling the blue lift. He noted a web of thin cirrus hanging over the far rim of the Valley. Further afield, a capstane of cloud lay on the braid shoothers of Tinto. A fresh sudron wind jinked through the trees. To the north, the Campsies, under the azure pool of the lift, wore their Spring livery as was only revealed on the clearest of days.
"Aye, rain later the day for shair," he mused.
He stravaiged on into the Moss, progressing by stepping from tuft to tuft, and so avoiding the worst of the waterlogged ground. Constantly, he kept

a wary eye open for the deep drainage channels which criss-crossed the Moss. Some of these were so steeply banked that it would be difficult to clamber out if one were to fall in. After a period of prolonged rainfall, the water could rise to a considerable depth, so that it would be very easy to drown, and in fact, this misfortune had happened to a few individuals in recent years.

However, as he gained somewhat drier ground he relaxed. He extracted the clay figurine from his one whole pocket and examined it fondly, stroking its contours. It was an extremely crude representation of a female figure, facial features harsh and angular. It was whole save for a missing left arm. No doubt this had been the treasured possession of a wee girl now long since dead.

Looking closer, he noticed a series of pinprick holes in the torso. A sudden thought occurred.

"Maybe this wis made by a wutch tae cast spells on her enemies."

The effigy seemed momentarily to twitch with life in his hand.

"Naw," he thought as he strolled on, still regarding it intently, "wutches just cast spells on dolls o wax."

Someone was watching him.

You know the feeling: the waiting for the imminent knife in the back; the bogle about to jump out on you from the trees, the shadowy figure behind you on the stairs, the murderer poised behind the door as you enter the darkened room.

Someone was watching him.

He froze, muscles seized momentarily, feeling the hot coal eyes questing amongst the very organs of his body. Wishing that his own eyes could migrate to the back of his head, he slowly inclined round. The Moss lay bare and menacing, but no sign of anyone.

The feeling lessened but did not completely subside as he scanned each side. Odd, this near forgotten primeval sense. He'd experienced it before, but never this strongly. He stared hard behind him. No, nothing; save for the ever freshening wind whisking the grass alive.

He turned to continue his wanderings, and was about to step forward when his leading boot felt the earth crumble beneath it. He leapt back as if stung. A deep drainage ditch yawned only inches in front of him. Its dark green watery depths beckoned. It occurred to him that he'd been so intent on the clay doll that if he hadn't experienced the oorie sensation of being watched then he would have fallen in.

"By God, ah'd have droont!" he breathed.

He regarded the doll with distaste. Its sharp features seemed to set in a malevolent grin. He abruptly dropped it involuntarily into the drainage ditch as if it were a venomous snake. It seemed to vanish into the peaty depths without a sound.

"A wutch's Stookie Wummin for shair!" He shivered to the marrow in terror and revulsion. "Ye'll bring me nae mair ill luck!"

He sidled away from the ditch, afraid to turn his back. When he could no longer see its lip he paused. He quivered uncontrollably for a moment; as if attempting to throw off the weird events of the past few moments.

He breathed deeply, then spun round in a panic. Nothing but wind and emptiness.

He realised that the feeling of being observed had gone. It was as if the staring eyes had closed, but uncannily he felt that they were but slumbering. He'd never been in this part of the Moss before; not that he could remember. The immediate area was featureless, save for a massive boulder on a knoll, and the eroded outline of an old peat bank nearby. He suddenly fled, like a deer which had just detected an unfamiliar and possibly threatening scent.

It was only after he had reached more familiar ground that he again reminded himself that if anyone had been watching him, they had saved him from at best a dooking and at worst from drowning.

He sat on the crest of a rise and eyed the increasingly steely western horizon. He reflected on what had been a morning that had far from lived up to its early promise. He wished now that he'd gone to school.

"Even auld Ridnose an aw thae toerags in ma class wid've been better than this," he concluded gloomily.

Still, what was done was done: besides he didn't have over long to go at the school. He was fourteen in ten days time and he could leave at Easter in two weeks. Good riddance to the place!

But he was astute enough to realise that leaving the school would only be exchanging one set of problems for another. He would have to earn his keep. His Stepfaither had boasted that he could get him started as a nipper down at the Stenton Steelworks.

"Aye," he'd said, " ye ken ah'm weel in wi the Manager o the Meltin Shop, done him a few favours, so ah huv. Tellt him aboot thon bluidy Communist McIntyre; him that wis tryin tae stir up trouble amongst the lads. Aye, he got his jotters guid an proper. Ah'll get ye in aw richt; mind ye'll huv tae haun in aw yer wages; ye're ower wee tae look efter yer money, ye'd juist spend it on books or some like rubbish."

Tommy knew fine that life as a nipper was no joke. You were like a slave, everybody bullied you; especially the other boys. Rab McKay kent a boy that had been a nipper: the other boys had stuck a red hot bolt down his breeks and it had burnt his erse rid raw, the courss bastards that they were. Somehow he had to escape the seeming inevitability of the future. Maybe he could run away to sea.

"Naw, naw, ah'll be a sodger like ma Da!"

The idea hit him and rolled through his mind infectiously.

"Aye, ah'll be a sodger. Ah'm ower young the noo, but when ah'm auld enough ah'll jine the Lanarkshire Yeomanry, then ah'll jine up wi the H.L.I, ma Da's auld regiment. Maybe they'll send me tae India, or Palestine, or even...Egypt." His eyes twinkled at the thought.

High on the knoll, observing the oncoming curtain of the rain, it was as if his future life had just clicked into place. The immediate future: mirk and threatening, like the grey veil of rain joining the land to the lift and concealing all in its wake. But somewhere, on the other side of the sky, there was light. It glimmered in his eyes.

A British Army Officer in pith helmet and tropical dress uniform wandered down the aisles of a long dead city of Colossi. The setting sun bathed the sand red as he paused to scan a hieroglyph. The tall, blond officer spun round as if called, his features glowed in a smile, and he held out his arms.

"Aye," murmured Tommy, "ah'm gaun tae be a sodger."

He caught sight of the Toun Knock and the spires of Wishie.

"Ah'll show yez aw!" he ground out, "ye that miscaw me, ah'll show yez, the keech that ye are. Ma mammy'll be fair proud o me then!"

CHAPTER 3

A muckle dreep of rainwater from an overflowing gutter overhead splooshed Tommy as he exited into Smith's Land from the close. It hardly mattered; by then he was absolutely drookit.
It was several hours later. He'd heard the Chapel Bell ring out four o' clock a short while before, so he was confident that he would arrive home at about the usual time; not that his Mother would be bothering anyway.
That afternoon he'd dilly-dallied vaguely homeward, in high spirits in spite of the worsening rain. He'd cut through the Co Creamery into Stewarton Street, then perched on top of the glass topped dyke at the Ginger Works, watching the loading and unloading of the carts, as the crates of empties were exchanged for hued crates of Vimto, Irn Bru, Cream Soda, and Ginger Beer. Eventually the yard foreman had hunted him.
He'd taken a brief stop to peer through the railings of the Academy as the straight ranks were marched through the Boys' Door at the end of the afternoon interval. From within emanated the martial strains of 'Scots Wi Hae'. The Heidie, Tommy knew, played the piano himself on an upper balcony as the weans filed to their classes.
He'd spent the rest of the afternoon at the Mercat. Nobody minded him. The sheds had been hoatching with fermers, ferm labourers and toon worthies, casting shrewd and often disparaging eyes on the quality of the beasts. The air was heavy with the guff of damp clothing, sawdust and hot sharn. Though he'd dried off somewhat in the sheds, he was soon drawn to the canny manoeuverings of the open air ring.
The bidders, or he assumed they were bidders, leaned nonchalantly on the pens. Some puffed idly at their baccy, some appeared almost asleep under their bunnets.
As some wild eyed beast cavorted daftly round the ring, harried this way and that by the Mercat drover, and the auctioneer's delivery rose to a crescendo, nary a sign of a bid could he see. When the hammer fell, hardly a sign of emotion could be detected; save for a slight relaxation in the shoothers of some, or a humph of irritation muttered almost under the breath.

Now Tommy opened the door to his house with some delicacy, and made a bee-line for the fire. A pan of tatties bubbled on the range.

He kicked off his boots across the room, then thinking better of it, retrieved them and placed them carefully by the grate. Then he perched on the edge of the fireplace feeling the sooty warmth seep into him. At first the dampness formed a cloaking layer between his skin and the heat, but gradually it seemed to melt away and his skin prickled in the luxury of the sudden warmth.

There was never a shortage of coal in the household; though never a penny did his stepfather pay to the local coalmen. It was as if their bunker was under a sorcerer's spell, and replenished itself as if by magic. In fact, Big Geordie and his crony, Gerry McCourt sneaked over to the Coalry at dead of night with a barrow and helped themselves.

Before each nocturnal expedition they slipped the auld watchman a shilling, and in return he made sure that he and his dogs were safely ensconced in his hut at the agreed time of the incursion.

When Tommy's back was as hot as a pie from a baker's oven, he birled round like a willing fowl on a spit. A damp wisp of steam from his jersey danced in the air almost immediately.

"Haw, get back frae thon fire! How many times dae ah huv tae tell ye. Ye're blockin aw the heat oot frae the hoose!"

A smartly dressed lady was glaring at him as he spun round.

Tommy blinked, "Maw, whit've ye done tae yer hair?"

A faint smile played about her freshly painted lips. She stroked her new hair do lightly.

"D'ye like it?" she pouted," it's the new Eugene Permanent Wave. Ah got it done at Buchanan's for only a guinea. It'll last me for the rest o the year."

"Jings oh, Maw, ye're a richt toff the day," declared Tommy, admiring the slim figure confronting him. Still relatively short for his age, Tommy was nonetheless an inch or so taller than his Mother. He studied the folds in her raven hair. They seemed to him like a section of a petrified sea. Her face was well powdered and rouged, but last night's bruise was still detectable. He noticed that she wore a new fur trimmed coat and commented on it.

"Aye, it's swell isn't it. Ah got it in the Co Drapery sale. It wis juist 39/6d. It'll go fine wi ma new hat. Aye, awthegither ah'll fair be able tae swank it doon Wishie Main Street."

She strolled ostentatiously to and fro.

"Ye're fair in the money this weather Maw," remarked Tommy, thinking about where the next meal was coming from.

She shrugged her shoulders. " The rent's peyed. Yer Faither got his overtime money at the end o last week."

"Ma Faither's deid!" snapped Tommy coldly.

She looked daggers at him. "Aye," she murmured, her expression softening momentarily. But then, as if remembering something, her features darkened once more, a belligerent look in her eyes.

"Whaur were ye the day?" she demanded.

"At the schule, whaur else?" Tommy mumbled, head down.

The side of his face seemed to explode as she skelped him a dull one. His head near jumped from his shoothers. The red brand of her palm glowed on his cheek.

"Ye leeir, the Attendance Officer was staunin on the step when ah came back frae the Hairdresser's. Whaur were ye?"

Still in a dwam, he spluttered out the truth. "Ah wis ower the Moss, Maw."

"Ah've tellt ye tae keep awa frae thon place. It's ower dangerous. Ye could faw doon a ditch an droon yersel."

"Aye, Maw," he hung his head, face still gouting at the blow.

"Weel, it's back tae Beltanfit the morn an six o the best frae the Maister. Aye, an it'll serve ye richt!"

She eyed him with distaste.

"Look at ye, ye're clairty as a Tink. An ye stink o coos an ferms!" She wrinkled her nose. "Ah'd be mortified tae be seen oot wi ye!"

Wounded to the marrow, he turned away and draped himself over the bunker by the window. He stared out misty eyed as the raindrops scrabbled down the panes.

"Awa oot tae the well an get some water. Ah'll shuin be gettin the plumber oot tae fix the pipe, sae ye'll no need tae dae it for much longer."

Unmoving, he stared at the useless Crane Tap.

" C'mon son. Get yersel washed; the tatties are ready," she coaxed, her temper abated. "Ah'll be buyin new claes next month, for when ye leave the schule; it'll no be ower lang noo, juist twa weeks."

Tommy,who'd heard this before, regarded her with mildly ironic eyes.

"Aye, Maw," he muttered, bending for the pail below the sink.

As he made to exit, she added,"An maybe yer Faither'll get ye a joab beside him richt enough."

Tommy stepped out into the rain, eyes haunted at the prospect.

CHAPTER 4

All that evening, the wind prowled like an angry river in spate, forming soft eddies then skelping through closes and round corners in berserk fury, firing keen slivers of icy water. It whomped doon the lum, causing the dulling embers of the fire to flare up into fresh life, and puff great gouts of smoky dragon's breath into the room.
Under the gutteral hiss of the flichterin mantle, Tommy sprawled over the rag rug in front of the fireplace. His Mother had gone off some time ago to the Williams' next door in order to show off her new hairdo.
In front of him was a neat display of the day's finds.
Pride of place went to a clay pipe head emblazoned with a shamrock. This, he reasoned, must have been owned by an auld Irish miner who had worked at one of the numerous auld pits fringing the area. Probably it had come over from Ireland. Below this were arranged the clay pipe stems; grouped into manufacturers: White, Coghill, Johnston; all known to him from previous discoveries.
He'd played himself in a game of Moshie with the four clay bools, experiencing that odd tingle he often felt when handling artifacts from the past. He had plunked one of the bools too hard, and it had skited off across the linoleum and under the sideboard. In the fitful light of the room, he'd been unable to find it. Not wishing to lose any more, he'd judged the game a bogey, and now the three remaining marbles were arranged in an equilateral triangle next to the two rows of potsherds. To achieve this optimum arrangement, he'd chopped and changed his display in pernickety fashion. Now he looked down with satisfaction.
The fire settled down in the grate and an ember cracked, spitting out a fizzing meteor up the lum. It was about time to put on more coal, but the scuttle was empty, and he was loathe to leave his cocoon of warmth to run the gauntlet of the rampaging storm outside in order to win his way to the coal cellar in the back court.
He rummaged below his bed for his shoe boxes in order to add his day's finds to them; but unwilling to break up his display just yet, he laid the boxes next

to the rug in readiness, reached for Volume 8 of his encyclopaedias, and settled down again.

As ever his eyes dwelt on the frontispiece illustration: 'Aborigines of South America'. This was a fine coloured engraving depicting the natives of Brazil, Patagonia and Tierra del Fuego. He looked longingly at the illustration of the Indian girl of the Botocudos Tribe, with her taut high breasts and wide hips tantalisingly bisected by a flimsy loin cloth. He felt a stirring within himself, then felt himself blushing, so he quickly flicked the pages over, and started to read at 'Smith, George, Assyriologist'.

There was a silence in the room save for the unending chorus of the raindrops flinging themselves at the panes and the grumble of the mantle. Deep in concentration, Tommy occasionally turned over a page as the fire shrunk even lower.

At the back of nine o clock, the room jerked into draughty animation as the door flew open. His mother subdued it as you would a frisky cuddy, and slammed it firmly shut. She shivered audibly.

"Whit a night! Ma new coat's near drookit juist frae next door!"

"Tommy, dinnae tell me ye've let the fire die doon. Ye're that busy wi yer auld books an jummle tae see whit's richt in front o yer neb! Richt, git roon tae the bunker an fou yon scuttle. Yer faither'll be in on tap o me lukin fur his tea, an ah huvnae struck a blow."

As Tommy rose with alacrity to comply, she added,"Aye, an when ye've feenisht that, redd up yer things, ah dinnae want ye under ma feet."

As the sirens denoting the end of the back shift ululated on the wind, the tatties were ready and the mince steamed in the pan. Obviously his Mother was pulling out all the stops to placate her husband in case he objected to her afternoon's spending spree.

It usually took Geordie scarcely ten minutes to hurry up from the Stenton, and, sure enough, the door was flung open by ten past ten. Geordie barged in.

"Hing on a wee minute, Wullie, an ah'll get ye it." He addressed an unseen compaion outside. with a brief nod to his wife, he strode over to the clock. He humphed in annoyance, finding nothing behind it.

"Haw Ag, whaur's ma pey envelope?"

Tommy, who had been sitting reading his encyclopaedia, could see the colour drain from his Mother's face, even beneath the rouge.

Geordie though, did not look at her, but without waiting for an answer

thrust open the top drawer of the sideboard and withdrew her purse.
"Whaur's the rest o ma pey?" he demanded, taking a florin from the purse.
"Ye cannae take that, ah need it for messages!" Agnes interjected desperately.
"Ah need it; Wullie's pitten it on a horse fur me the morn."
"Aye, but....."
"Oot ma road wummin." He shoved her roughly aside.
Approaching the door, he wrung the anger out of his face.
"Here ye are Wullie: see ye bring ma winnins tae me the morn's nicht, eh!" he exclaimed heartily.
"Aye we'll see," replied a retreating voice.
Geordie slammed the door. The anger rushed back over his features.
"Richt," he growled dangerously," whaur's ma pey envelope?"
He stalked towards her. Tommy nestled deep down into the chair, merging himself into it.
Realisation came into Geordie's eyes as he noticed his wife's hair for the first time.
"Oh aye, ah see whit ye've done wi it."
"D'ye no like it?" she chattered anxiously. "D'ye no want me tae look guid for ye? Come an sit doon; yer tea's ready."
Geordie, however, would not be sidetracked. He cut through her nervous babbling.
"Whaur's the rest? It disnae cost three pounds fur a hairdo!"
Her mouth set hard and she stood up straight, eyes piercing with determination. She made no reply.
In a fury, he grabbed her by the collar and pinned her against the wall.
"Whaur's the money!" he demanded.
"Get aff me!" Mustering all her strength, she heaved her shoulders and threw him off.
"Ah spent maist o it!" she spat out unapologetically.
"Ye whit!"
Fixing her collar, she glowered darkly at him.
"Ah spent it on a new coat for masel. It wis a bargain."
In instantaneous reaction, he lashed out at her, but she was quick enough to cover her head with her arms, and the heavy blow thudded against them. His hand drew back to strike her again.
At that point, Tommy's fear tipped over into reckless fury. Still clutching his encyclopaedia, he flew across the room. With all his strength, he walloped

his Stepfather on the back of the head with the heavy book, which bounced out of his hands with the force of the impact. The big man staggered, lost his balance, and clattered against the wall. Dazed, he slowly slid to the floor. After a moment, he shook his head, and started to heave himself up.
"Leave her alane, ye auld bastard!"
Tommy hurled himself at him again, fists flailing. Caught by surprise once more, Geordie couped over under the rain of blows. His nose started to bleed copiously.
Agnes, who had watched the tableau unfold with horrified amazement, darted between them. Shoving Tommy away, she wailed, "Naw, Son, he'll hauf kill ye!"
Tommy blinked, as if snapping out of a trance; the awful realisation of what he had done suddenly dawning on him.
With a deep growl, Geordie once more started to get to his feet. Tommy and his Mother stood transfixed. Geordie dabbed at the hot blood channeling over his lips, then roared towards Tommy, arming his Wife aside.
Tommy attempted to take last minute avoiding action, but was too late. His Stepfather clattered into him, sending him hurtling across the room. He careered into the table, which toppled over. The centre of the room erupted into a whirling mass of somersaulting table legs, limbs and china bowls.
His first rush of anger spent, a twisted smirk spread across Geordie's features as he surveyed the quivering figure of Tommy extricating himself from the wreckage.
"Noo ye're for it, ye wee shite!" he leered, eyes glinting at the prospect of the systematic beating he was about to inflict.
As he advanced on the wild eyed boy, his eye settled on the encyclopaedia with which Tommy had struck him. He scooped it up from the floor and flexed his arm to fling it at Tommy, but halted in mid action. He smirked once more.
"Ye an yer bluidy books, ah'll show ye whit they're guid for!" He inclined towards the fire.
"Naw Geordie," screeched Agnes, "ye cannae dae that; it belanged tae his Faither!" She vainly attempted to grab the volume from his hand.
The force of his wrath seemingly having been transferred from her, Geordie contented himself by barring her way with his free arm.
"Keep oot o this, Hen." He knew he was firmly in command again.
Deftly, he wheiched the book into the fire.

Tommy screamed in mortal agony as if it was his very flesh that was in contact with the red hot coals. With a sob he darted to the fire, plucking at the book, but involuntarily drew back from the intense heat, so that he merely suceeded in flicking it over, so exposing the inside to the flames. He frantically dipped his hand in the volcano once more, and the book, now partially aflame, tumbled on to the grate. it opened at the frontispiece. He watched in despair as a tongue of flame crept up the thighs of the Indian Maiden.

"That'll teach ye!" guffawed Geordie, stepping towards him once more.

"Naw, dinnae hit him any mair!" begged Agnes, rooted fearfully to the spot. Tommy looked up, eyes demonic with fury. He snatched up the pan of steaming mince and launched it at his Stepfather.

Geordie howled in prolonged agony as it struck him a glancing blow on the side of the face and coated him with a viscous boiling mass. Blubbering, he fell to his knees as he scrabbled to scrape off the scalding mince with the lapel of his jacket.

Mouth agape at his atrocious act, Tommy stood hypnotised, like a child observing the death agonies of a wasp which has just been swatted. His Mother shook him vigorously.

"Run Son, git oot o here or he'll kill ye for shair!"

He gazed at her gowk-like for an instant, then skelped out of the door.

The Wind bore him along on its mighty shouthers, scraiching like the Deil; then tantalising him, set up a great wall against him at the Close. Breath squashed out of him, he won the street. He belted a zig-zag path along West Thornlie Street, then up Russell Street out of sight. Great bestial gasps of his pursuer seemed to rasp in his ears.

The Wind his ally again, he shot through a tenement close, across a back court, and louped the dyke into the grounds of the Methodist Kirk. In the darkness, he misjudged his jump, and landed awkwardly. His brow jarred the wet ground, and he lay partially stunned for a moment. He came to and turned over. The night sky was aflame with stars, glaring down at him like lunatic eyes. The wind was drawing aside the vast black curtain of storm, and the rain had ceased. No threatening footsteps approached.

"Aw naw, ah've killt him," the thought reared in his mind. "Naw, couldnae, have, but he'll murder me."

He bit his lip in distraction. Where could he go?

A great star flichtered like a wind-whisked fire near the Western horizon.

The connection established itself in his mind.

"Hairy Wullie. Aye Hairy Wullie!" he half shouted in relief. "He aye keeps his fire burnin intae the nicht."

Hairy Wullie lived in a crude, self constructed hovel on the fringes of the Moss between Waterloo and Lochview. He was a Daftie; folk said he wasn't all there. It was rumoured that he was the gowk son of a family in Waterloo, and had been cast out to live rough, though it was said that at dead of night his mother crept over the Moss with food: either that or he was fed by bogles.

Though wild and tousy, with straggly hair and beard, he was a youngish man who'd grown hard and muscular through digging for peat. He had his own unofficial banks on land owned by the Peat Company. Neither Gerry Rolink who worked for the Company, nor Buck Jones the Gamey minded him.

In fact, Hairy Wullie was widely tolerated. In Winter, when there was no peat to sell, he'd go round the doors selling firewood from offcuts from Rae's Sawmill, buying rags, selling stookie for steps, sharpening knives or telling fortunes. Folk said he had 'The Sight', and to be sure it was a brave householder who would set their dug on him, or child who would shout after him.

Hairy Wullie would just stand and stare in his daft way, and in an instant, so it seemed, the tyke would calm and slink off, the child's tongue would still or the offending householder would feel a questing inside their skull, then a peace.

Some older folk made the sign of the Evil Eye as he passed; many held that he could put a curse on folk who mistreated him. At any rate, daft or not, he made enough from his hawking to live on, and whether or not the tales of clandestine visitations by night were true, he managed to feed himself adequately.

Tommy had befriended him the previous Summer, whilst digging at the small coup by Waterloo. Engrossed in his task, he'd been unaware of the figure keenly observing at his shoulder. Like most local children, Tommy had previously given Hairy Wullie a wide berth, and had started with fear when the queer, bird like voice asked him what he was howking for. But when he'd observed the serene face regarding him beneath the hair and muck, he'd extracted some of his discoveries from his pocket and held them out wordlessly.

"They're bonnie," Wullie had said," an ah ken whaur ye'll find mair."
A queer friendship had sprung up between them from that point, which was considerably consolidated when Wullie revealed the existence of a hitherto unknown coup near a ruined cottage, where Tommy had made the best of his finds until the site became exhausted.

Now it was to Hairy Wullie that he'd fly: one outcast to another.

Momentarily the Wind held a dark cry and Tommy fled over the Kirk wall and up Caley Road into Stewarton Street. The wind and rain had scoured the street clear of folk; there was only the occasional huddle in a doorway or close. A light showed in the Market Bar, but the doors had long since been barred.

Since he had a fair way to go, Tommy initiated his standard method of progress when travelling a distance; run three lamposts, walk one. This formula had served him well when in a hurry in a built up area. He inhaled deeply, then set off.

In no time, he'd reached the boundary wall of the Ginger Works. Arms on hips, he paced its length, feeling the rush of his pulse ease to a steady flow. At the corner of Greenhead Road, the limit of the street lighting, he paused to cast anxious eyes up the empty expanse of the street behind him, then launched himself into the great pool of night between Greenhead and Waterloo Cross.

Peching, he stopped at the top of the brae several hundred yards further on, and surveyed the view behind as he fought for breath.

Stewarton Street, said to have been a Roman Road, marched straight as a die to the Cross and the Toon Knock beyond. From the murky line of starlit gloom near at hand to the grey moth flicker of the streetlit portion, it was devoid of any soul. The town wore a warm orange halo, like some outpost of Hell, as the furnaces of the Lanarkshire or the Stenton filled the night with their angry glower.

But here at the top of the brae there was only the night, chill and dreich. A filmy brig, star-rivetted, spanned the great arch of the lift from one horizon to another.

Tommy yawned deeply then trotted off, heading for the beckoning lights of Waterloo.

Soon he could distinguish the vague spark of a fire as he progressed along the Newmains Road just north of Waterloo Cross. Wullie's hut was screened from the road by a small plantation, but the fire winked through its depths.

He knew the ground well, even though he had never approached the hut by night, so he cut off the road and skirted the plantation with a confident stride. He knew of no bogs or drainage channels in the immediate vicinity. The fire reared up at him as he crept near. The hovel hunched in on itself like a humphy backit man in slumber.

"Wullie, are ye there?" he hissed in an anxious whisper.

The fire crackled ahint him, but no sound escaped from the dreaming hovel.

"Wullie, it's me, Wee Tam." Louder this time.

Silence.

"Wullie!" he yelled near to panic. Then there was a figure standing at his shoulder.

He scraiched in terror, and tottered back towards the fire. Hands big as shovels grasped him firmly and pulled him back. Eyes soft as moonlight shone down at him from a tousy face.

"Jeez oh Wullie, ah ver near endit masel!" Tommy exhaled in a rush of relief.

"Naw, naebodie kens when ah'm aboot." The piping tone was disconcerting, as was the fact that the movement of the lips was scarcely detectable under the mat of facial hair.

"Ye're in bother then," he continued. It was more a statement of fact than a question.

"Aye, how did ye ken?"

Wullie made no response, but turned and glowered into the darkness, listening intently. Tommy gawked into the dowie mirk of the Moss. There was nothing there; he could hear nothing, but he kept on staring till the black depths of the Moss seemed to merge into the starlit sky. The darkness clutched at him. The fire whoomed as a sudden gout of wind sent a sheeny cloud of sparks scrabbling at him.

He shook himself free of the dark. Lack of sleep was catching up with him, he thought.

Wullie too, had averted himself from the night and was warming himself by the fire, which was imprisoned in a rusty old brazier. He regarded Tommy with a penetrating stare, which Tommy found most off-putting.

"Ma Stepfaither was gaun tae batter ma Maw, so ah clouted him wan," mumbled Tommy by way of a considerably simplified explanation of his presence.

"He's gaun tae fair murder me when he gets me. Can ah bide the nicht wi ye, ah've naewhere else tae go?"

Hairy Wullie blinked. His expression was still grim.
"Whitever the reason, ye were called here the nicht. Aye ye can stey."
Tommy wrinkled his brow, "Whit d'ye mean?"
But Wullie had lumbered into his hut.
"By here, he's got some queer notions, but ye cannae expect anythin else frae a daftie," thought Tommy.
Wullie had drawn aside the old door which was propped over the entrance, and as Tommy entered the big man replaced it, shutting out the night. Only slivers of firelight showed through the irregular joins in the wall timbers. Most of the planks had been obtained somehow or other from Rae's Sawmill at Waterloo, and the results of Wullie's labours seemed solid enough.
Tommy had been inside the hut before, and so was prepared for the powerful stench of unwashed clothes and mouldy straw. The earth floor was covered with part of an old tarpaulin and crumbling lengths of linoleum. In one corner were mounds of straw, dried peat and torn blankets; at the opposite end was a worm eaten chair. Between these landmarks, a clamjamphrie of sacks, rusty tools, storage jars, pans and rough crockery were scattered willy-nilly. Incongruously, a grubby china doll peeked out above a cream jug.
A cruisie lamp burned on the chair, giving the illusion of cosiness, but a thousand draughts hissed through the fabric of the hut, needling Tommy from all angles. He chittered uncontrollably, the heat generated from his run now evaporated.
"Richt, ower there," Wullie gestured to the mound of straw.
Tommy buried himself in the rancid depths. Wullie piled all of the blankets over him, then scooped a mass of straw and peat into the centre of the floor. Caunnily, he laid out the biscuity rectangles of peat then heaped the straw.
"Take wan o ma blankets, ye've left yersel nane," offered Tommy.
"Naw, naw, ah'm yased tae the cauld; ah'm oot in aw weathers ye ken. Anywey," he continued, rummaging behind the chair, "Ah've got ma goonie!"
To Tommy's amazement, he produced a long white night gown, and donned it on top of his tattered overcoat. Wullie giggled, then buried himself in the straw.
In spite of his total exhaustion, sleep did not come easily to Tommy. The dampness of the ground seemed to wash up into his very bones. His bruises gowped. The day's events dissolved, then reformed themselves, altered beyond recognition.

A body floated in an icy pool, face down, flesh in slimy tatters. Inexorably it turned over. Face undecayed, he smiled up at himself. The visage screamed in laughter; but the voice was Geordie's.

Geordie lay in the fireplace, shrieking on a bed of coals. His feet were aflame. The snarling, fiery tongues crept slowly up his legs. Suddenly, he leapt up from the fire, tottered on charred legs, and came at him, een coruscating with death.

Tommy was anchored to the spot, a pair of muckle hands thrappling him. Geordie's torso continued to be consumed, until a blackened animated corpse compressed his neck to a scrawny bane.

But there, in the corner, a shadowy figure observed. Even as the life was being worried out of him, Tommy gawked at the shadow. Faceless, it seemed to beckon, and the death grip round his throat dissolved to the chill reality of the gloomy hut.

Tommy, instantly awake, sat bolt upright.

"Wullie, were ye ower the Moss the day?"

Wullie grunted, dopey with sleep.

"Were ye watchin me ower the Moss the day?"

"Aye," yawned a sleep filled voice, "ah wis ower the Moss."

"Aye but, were ye watchin me? Where were ye?" continued Tommy, somewhat exasperated.

Wullie chose to answer the latter question. "Just roon aboot here, an doon by the Waterloo Coup."

"So ye couldnae have been watchin me? Ye didnae see me the day, did ye?"

"Naw, ah didnae see ye. How? Were ye ower the Moss the day?"

" Aye!" Tommy clicked his tongue with irritation. Wullie was really saft in the heid at times.

"Ah spent ver near the hale day up at the Moss Coup and on the Moss. But there wis somebody spyin on me."

"Did ye mak oot who it wis?"

"Naw, if ah'd hae seen who it wis, ah widnae be askin ye if ye were watchin me, would ah?"

"Naw, ah dinnae think ye would," said Wullie slowly. "How d'ye ken ye were bein watched?" he continued, worming out the weak point in Tommy's statements.

"Ah could feel it, richt in ma banes. Ye juist ken thae kind o things."

"Aye, ah ken fine whit ye mean. Ah'm aye gettin thae feelins masel."

Wullie was totally convinced.

"Wis this aside the muckle stane?" he demanded.

"Whit stane?"

"Juist a muckle stane, aw on its ain, atap a wee hillock, wi nae plantation near haund."

"Aye, there wis a stane, a muckle freestane." A note of panic crept into Tommy's voice.

"An ye didnae see him?"

"Whit d'ye mean? Ah tellt ye ah saw naebodie!"

"Ah dinnae gang ower that wey!" snapped Wullie.

Tommy was baffled at the turn of the conversation. A silence cloaked the hut as he tried to grasp the implications of what his friend had said. He shook his head. 'Naw,' he reasoned to himself,' he disnae unnerstaun whit ah'm askin o him: he'll say the first thing that comes intae his heid. He kin be as twistit as a coarkscrew. He's a guid sowl, but ah've got tae mind that he's juist a gowk. But how did he ken that it wis near the stane?'

"Ah ken whit ye're thinkin," intoned Wullie abruptly. "Ye think ah'm aw blethers, but ye'll be back tae find oot mair aboot yon place!"

There was a hurt silence, then he blurted out, "He cries oot tae me ye ken, but ah dinnae listen. He wis cryin oot the nicht, but it wisnae tae me, it wis tae you!"

"Who's cryin oot?" demanded Tommy, but Wullie, in the strunts, turned over and buried himself in the straw.

Though his nerves were jangling, Tommy pressed him no further, well aware that when Wullie went into one of his thrawn moods he just had to be left alone. 'Ah'll get the answer oot o him in the mornin,' he reasoned confidently.

Outside the rain battered against the hovel from all sides once more, and a fine spray wafted in from the doorway. Tommy cooried down as the rain's staccato filled the night.

CHAPTER 5

Tommy awoke, the Wind gossiping in his ears. The tip of his neb nipped with the cold, but the rest of him was bathed in a comfy, sweaty warmth. No sound of rain on the roof. He turned over and eased his head out of the straw. The hut was deserted, and the door had been hauled away from the entrance. Outside, the Moss glowed in a pool of sun, then blinked out as a grey cloud shadow linked past the hut.
He sat up and stretched, still in an envelope of heat. As he picked the straw from his hair and jersey, he noticed a bowl with a small jug and spoon beside him. The bowl was filled nearly to the brim with parritch and there was some milk in the jug. The parritch was long cold. He sniffed at the milk. It smelt fresh. Wullie must have fetched it that very morning. As he gazed at the parritch, the hunger snarled in his belly, and without further hesitation, he upended the jug into the parritch and wolfed in.
In a minute flat, the bowl lay empty beside him. He stood up, grimacing in the draught from the doorway, and dusted himself off again. There was a stiffness in his limbs and his back was a girdle of pain where he'd collided with the table. His cheek felt tender and swollen.
Dangling from a nail in the wall above the old chair was a small mirror. The glass below a diagonal crack had fallen out, so that only a triangle of glass remained. He moved towards it, wondering idly what Wullie would want with a mirror. The mirror was too high for him: he could just see the upper part of his face when he stood on his tiptoes.
Looking around, he seized a battered enamel chanty, upended it, and perched on top. The face of a clairty tink stared back at him. He winced at his own appearance. Though he was fairly casual about washing, and cared little about his general appearance, he had never seen himself in such a state. Two red-rimmed eyes stared at him below a spiky haystack of dirty fair hair. Even the muck and grime caking his features could not conceal the puffy stain of bruised blood where his mother had slapped him.
"Jeez oh, ah must be honkin," he breathed.
He sniffed under his oxters, then shrugged his shoulders; he couldn't detect

anything particularly malodorous; maybe the general background guff inside the hut had deadened his sense of smell.

He grimaced crookedly at himself

'Ma Maw wis richt enough when she called me a tink,' he thought to himself.

At the thought his face fell as he recalled the perilous situation in which he had left his mother.

"Whit's happened tae ma Mammy!"

He skelped out through the doorway, but the blaze of sunlight started him out of his momentary mad breinge, and forced him to consider the best way forward.

He inhaled a draught of brisk air and took stock of the weather.

Great white citadels of cloud were being precipitated across a backcloth of northern blue by a keen north-west wind. He could see clearly that some dragged huge rainy trunks behind them, dowsing the land in icy squalls. The Sun flashed in and out of existence at their passage.

This was the weather he liked. He cast off the chill and took another greedy lungful of air. Now he could focus on his dilemma.

Should he go back to the house, and if so when?

Feeling the pressure in his bladder he relieved himself, pissing into the heart of the fire, as if attempting to extinguish the troubles that flamed in his mind.

He'd have to go back to find out what had happened, but clearly he'd have to ensure that his stepfather was not around when he did so. Geordie was on Back Shift that week, so provided his burns were not too severe, the coast would be clear for him to return to the house after about quarter to two.

He'd no means of knowing the time at that moment. It felt late. He looked around. There was no sign of Wullie anywhere. The only sign of human activity was a sooty serpent of smoke coiling from the Brickit Works beyond the Plantation. He looked harder, then caught a flicker of movement. A figure carrying a spade over his shoulder was plodding towards the peat banks by Lochview.

"That'll be Gerry startin, so it cannae be ower late," he reasoned.

Clearly he still had time to kill. On an impulse, he decided to go and watch Gerry Rolink at work; perhaps he let him help. Gerry lived with his father, mother, brother and five sisters in Moss Cottage close to Waterloo. His father, now well advanced in years, was the foreman of the Moss Litter

Company. Gerry, though no Spring Chicken himself, now carried out the bulk of the heavy work.

He'd meant to question Wullie further about his strange remarks of the night before, but that obviously would have to wait. No doubt he'd see him soon.

Before leaving, he nosed around the hovel, making doubly sure that Wullie was not concealing himself inside for some mysterious purpose. The empty porridge bowl prickled a small question. There was no sign of a porridge pot in the hut or by the fire, so how had Wullie made the porridge. Where had it come from?

He crunkled his brow. Perhaps someone had brought it to him. Maybe the stories were true. He shook his head in mystification and set off at a daunner towards the peat hag.

CHAPTER 6

Betty McKay peched up the last of the Station Steps. Slightly small and plump for her twelve and a half years, she was somewhat red faced with the effort. She felt fair wearit: it had not been one of her better days. The Sewing Mistress, Auld Fanny Bryce, had given her two of the tawse for what she considered shoddy work. The injustice of it still rankled.
She gasped for air at the top of the steps and glowered back at Beltanfit Schule. Then her expression softened. A twinkle came into her eyes. She dropped her school bag and took a furtive keek to left and right. Seeing no one, she took a running jump at the high parapet of the railway bridge and bunked herself up, so that she balanced on the parapet at waist height. She scanned the Kye's Entry just beyond the brig.
Her face glowed with satisfaction. Her Father had been away on a long drove, the last part of which involved bringing a goodly herd of stirks down to the station. Sure enough the stirks were there, docile in their pens. Her Father was home again.
Abruptly, a pair of hands clutched her by the waist.
"Ye're fawin!" bowfed a voice. Betty scraiched out in surprise, then let herself dreep off the parapet.
"Ye eejit!" she snapped at the shabby figure grinning at her.
"How ye daein, Betty Bumbee?" smirked Tommy.
"Aw richt, Smelly Nellie!" she returned.
She was a spirited lass, quite capable of sticking up for herself. She regarded him with distaste: he looked as though he'd been dragged through a hedge backwards.
"Ye're manky Tommy, whit've ye been daein wi yersel?" She held her nose in mock disgust.
"Och, ah've been up Greenheid Moss," he shrugged.
"Ye've been plunkin the schule again, the Attendance Officer's been at yer door. Ma Mammy saw him this mornin!"
"Aye ah ken," said Tommy nonchalantly," he wis there yesterday an aw."
"Ye've got a brass neck, but ye'll fair catch it frae Auld Ridnose when ye go

34

back!" declared Betty knowingly.

"Aye well, it's nothin ah havnae had afore."

Changing the subject he asked, " Anywey ye werenae lookin ower happy comin up thae stairs. Wis the effort ower much for ye?"

"Naw it wisnae. Ah got twa o it frae Auld Fanny Bryce this efternin, if ye want tae ken. Auld bitch; ah've tellt her that ah cannae sew properly because o ma twa thumbs that ah broke when ah wis a bairn, but she'll no listen tae me. Anywey that disnae matter; ma Da's hame again!"

They strolled up past the Coalry. Tommy dilly-dallied as they approached Girdwood's and the close mouth leading to Smith's Land. It was time to ask the favour he sought. In truth he had been waiting for Betty for the last half hour.

"Betty, hing on a meenit. There's been trouble at hame."

"Aye, ah kent ye were in bother. The hale buildin heard aw the cafuffle. It must've been some rammy. Ma Mammy looked oot o the windae an saw ye tankin oot o the hoose , an a meenit later she saw yer Stepfaither howlin blue murder, rinin efter ye through the close, cursin an sweirin. He didnae get ye, did he?" She scanned his features appraisingly.

"Naw, but he'll murder me when he does! Listen, would ye dae me a favour?"

"Whit favour?" She regarded him with suspicion. She'd been well warned not to get involved in family rows between Geordie Brawley and the Neills.

"Ah want tae find oot if ma Maw's aw richt, but ah need tae make sure that Big Geordie's no in. Would ye go tae ma door and find oot for me?" Tommy looked pleadingly at her.

"How will ah ken if he's no in if yer Mammy comes tae the door?"

"Juist say that yer Da wants a word wi him, or somethin."

"Ma Da cannae stick Big Geordie, he widnae gie him the time o day!"

"Say anythin ye like, juist find oot!"

Betty looked doubtful.

"Ah'm gaun tae buy some Soor Plooms. Ah'll share them wi ye," he coaxed.

"Where would you git money for sweeties? Ye've never any money."

He held out a penny halfpenny. "Ah wis helpin Gerry Rolink up at the Peats. He gave me this."

Betty thought hard. She was particularly fond of Soor Plooms and had not tasted any for many a day.

"Aye aw richt, ah'll dae it. But first ah'm gaun in tae see ma Da. Go doon by the Station Steps, an ah'll see ye in aboot hauf an hour."

Tommy draped himself over the parapet of the bridge as he waited After a time the signal on the Up Line to Lanark flipped up. He peered down the line. It did not take him long to distinguish a moving oblique linetrail of smoke by the Battleaxe Sweet Works. The rails started to hum and the train appeared round the bend. It lumbered into the station with an armoured snort. As the engine rumbled under the brig, he was enveloped in a gush of grimy, dank vapours; the delicious stink of trains that spoke of travel and far off places. As it protested to a rending halt, several doors sprang open, and a few assorted travellers emerged. A fusillade of slammed doors beat out a rhythm against the waiting hiss of the fretty engine. A whistle, then the carriages squeaked, and with great sooty wuffs the train lurched forwards. Tommy dreeped off the parapet and darted over to the other side to watch. The dirl of the train gradually faded.

"Haw, ah've been lookin for you!" A deep voice behind him.

He louped backwards with fright, lost his footing, and clattered down on his dowp.

"Aye, twa can play at that gemme!" giggled a girl's voice.

Betty McKay grinned fit to burst. Revenge was sweet.

"Ye besom ye!" Tommy picked himself up. " Ma erse is gowpin!" he moaned.

" Did ah gie ye a wee fright son?" boomed Betty in a fair impression of a man's voice. She hooted in laughter.

Tommy grinned sheepishly.

"Well, did ye find oot?"

" Aye, he's awa tae work. It's juist yer Mammy that's in."

"Does she look aw richt?" he asked anxiously.

"Aye, a bit doon in the mooth maybe, but that's aw," she replied.

Tommy exhaled in relief.

" And that's no aw," beamed Betty, " ah've another bit o guid news!" She paused, building up the suspense.

" Well, are ye gaun tae tell me?" blurted out Tommy impatiently

" Oor Rab's hame. He ran awa frae the ferm."

" By here, that is guid news." Tommy's face glowed with pleasure. "But will he no get intae trouble?" he added doubtfully.

" Ma Da gave him a richt bleachin for runnin awa, but then Rab tellt him aboot whit had been happenin. They ver near worked him tae death, ye should see his haunds. He's juist a rickle o banes; it's awfie tae see him. Aw he got tae eat wis breid an parritch. The other boays were aye tryin tae get him tae dae their work. They bullied him when he widnae dae it. As weel as that the grieve would aye clip his lugs or dunt him wan tae mak him hurry. Ma Da wis fair mad when he tellt him, so he said that he disnae need tae go back; he wis near the end o his term anyway. Next time ma Da sees yon fermer at the Feein Mercat at Lanark he says he's gaun tae gie him a piece o his mind."

" Where's Rab noo?"

" Him an ma Da are stickin in tae a big plate o stovies. He'll be oot in a wee while."

"That's guid, tell him ah'll see him later. Richt, ah'd better awa in an see ma Maw."

He edged off in the direction of home.

Betty stood still, hands on hips,"Ye're forgettin somethin are ye no?"

"Whit?"

Ye were gaun tae share yer sweets wi me," she grinned astutely.

"Aye, richt ye are." Tommy had genuinely forgotten. "C'mon intae Ikey Moses's."

The bell tingled as they entered the shop vauntily. There were no other customers. A wee shilpit man with a prominent nose peered at them over the counter.

" Ah've nae misshapes the day, sae ye neednae ask." He spoke in a nebby wee voice.

Ikey Moses was well known for his meanness; there was no tick allowed in his shop.

Tommy puffed himself up to his full five feet two inches.

"Ah'm no wantin a farthin's worth o yer auld misshapes; ah'm in for Soor Plooms. He held out his penny halfpenny haughtily. Betty guffawed behind his back.

"Oh aye, in the money the day are we?" The ghost of a grin brushed over the wee man's features.

" Aye, ah'm fair the toff the day." Tommy raised his nose appreciably.

" Stick a pin intae him an he'll bust," commented Betty with a laugh.

Tommy turned and regarded her coldly, but said nothing.

Ikey weighed out the soor plooms carefully till the pan with the sweets seemed barely level with the weighted one, then he tumbled them into a bag.

He was about to hand it over, when he stopped and looked furtively at the door leading to the back shop. Seeing no one, he plunged his hand into the jar and extracted several more green balls which he secreted into the bag so swiftly that Tommy believed he had imagined it.

"There ye are, a penny halfpenny's worth o Soor Plooms," he announced, his features expressionless.

Outside the shop, Betty, whose cheeks were already bulging with a sooker, jabbed a thumb in the direction of Ikey, " Ye ken, He's no sae measly at aw."

" Ah ken, it's no true whit folk say aboot him. He whiles gies me misshapes for nothin."

" Aye me tae, he wis aye giein me some when ma Da wis oot o work."

" It's yon wife o his that's the mean yin, she's a fair tartar, an he' richt feart o her."

"He's juist a puir wee sowl!" said Betty with feeling, " Ah feel that vexed for him when she gies him a sherrackin in front o the customers in the shop."

"Tommy nodded his agreement as they entered the close. Betty lived upstairs two houses along, and so entered her house by the stairs in the back court. Impatient to see his mother, Tommy rushed off calling, "If everythin's aw richt ah'll be oot in aboot hauf an hour tell Rab!"

On reaching the door, he decided that it would be prudent to take precautions against the unlikely possibility that Betty had been mistaken. Accordingly, he knocked firmly, but hung back from the door, the balls of his feet tensed to spirit him away.

The door flew open," Ah'm scunnered wi....." an irate Agnes stopped in mid tirade.

Relief glowed in her face," Son, are ye aw richt. Ah wis fair worried aboot ye! Ah thocht it wis yon auld crabbit bugger o an Attendance Officer again. C'mon in!"

Tommy hesitated. He scanned her face, searching for tell tale signs of a beating. Her face seemed unmarked, save for the ghost of the bruise of two nights before.

"Are ye aw richt Maw?" he enquired anxiously, as if unable to believe the evidence of his own eyes.

" Aye, ah'm fine Son, Come on in, there's naebody in but me."

Still Tommy hung back. " He didnae batter ye, did he?"

" Naw, naw," she stepped out and shepherded him inside.

" He widnae really batter me ye ken," she said reassuringly.

" Awa ye go Maw. Ah ken fine he's aye hittin ye."

Tommy glared at her, hatred for his stepfather welling to the surface.

" Och, ah can haunnle that yin, he's easy enough dealt wi, it's no the first time ah've gied him a dull yin back," she grinned.

" Have ye Maw?" asked Tommy admiringly.

" Och aye, ah ken where tae hit him. There's weys o dealin wi a man ye ken." Her grin broadened.

" An he didnae hit ye last night when he couldnae catch me?"

A cloud of disbelief still clung to Tommy.

" Naw. Richt enough he wis dancin mad when he came back, but ah soon quietened him down. Ah gave him two bottles o beer ah had planked, an ah tellt him ah wid take ma new coat back."

" That's a sin Maw, ye looked that swanky in it."

" Ah weel, there'll be other coats, ah shouldnae have bocht it in the first place."

She humphed. " Aye, ah had a gey hard time gettin them tae gie me the money back tae: wee neb o a lassie wisnae gaun tae gie me it, but ah said ah'd caw for the manager and cause a cafuffle, so she gied me it then."

She sighed, " Aye, it wis a bonnie coat."

The dreamy look disappeared from her face. " Where did ye get tae last night?" she demanded.

" Up the Moss. Ah've got a pal that bides there. He let me stey wi him in his wee hut."

She sniffed, "Ah might've kent. C'mon noo and get washed, yer like a tattie bogle."

He bent down automatically to extract the pail from below the sink.

" Ye neednae bother wi that, Son!" She regarded him with a triumphant expression. " The plumber's been this mornin; the pipes are sortit."

With a look of wonder, Tommy gingerly turned on the Crane tap. Life bubbled in it hesitantly; it gouted a little, then gushed forth a steady stream. Tommy gawked like a primitive tribesman who had just seen his first motor car.

"Come oan, dinnae juist staun an look at it, get yon auld jersey aff and get washed; an nane o yer coo's licks either!"

He removed his jersey and flung it on the floor. His Mother grabbed it with distaste and rolled it into a ball.

" Richt this is for the Coup!" She flung it at the door.

" But Maw ah havnae another yin!" protested Tommy.

She looked at him teasingly. "Naw? Whit's this then?"
She crunkled open a brown paper parcel and held up a new woollen jumper.
" Is it for me?"
" Aye, course it is! Ah said ah'd get ye new claes. Ah bocht it wi some o the money ah got back for ma coat. It wis in the sale, it wis a bargain; juist 3/11d. Ah'll get ye new breeks and bits next month for when ye leave the schule."
" Thanks Maw!"
She shrugged. " Noo get washed, an dinnae forget yer legs an body."
Feeling as fresh as a daisy, Tommy dried himself off by the fire. His Mother sat on the armchair and watched him with a solemn expression.
" Noo Son," she broached the inevitable subject, " ye cannae stey here the nicht."
Tommy looked stoic, " Ah ken that ."
" Ah calmed yer Faither doon, but he says he owes ye a bleachin. He's got a gey sair face, wan side o it wis aw burnt as rid as a beetroot."
" Ah dinnae care. Serves the auld bastard right!"
" Watch yer sweirin!" his Mother reprimanded automatically.
" He burnt ma Da's book." He gazed wistfully into the fire.
His Mother's expression softened. " Aye ah ken whit it meant tae ye."
Like salt thrown on the fire, Tommy's temper raged.
" Naw ye don't, ye didnae care aboot ma Da; ah heard ye sayin it tae ma Granda!" He flung the accusation in her face.
" That's no true!"
Hurt overwhelmed her and she turned away, burying her head in her hands. Muffled sobs emerged.
He bit his lip, regretting his outburst. He recalled the tears in her eyes as they'd seen the Remembrance Day parade go by the previous year.
She wiped her eyes and turned to face him. A tear still channelled down her cheek.
" Aye ah cared for him, yer ower young tae unnerstaun!"
" Well whit d'ye stey wi Big Geordie for?"
" He's ma man," she returned simply.
" Noo Son," the urgency of the present situation re-impressed itself on her,
" ye cannae stey here the nicht, yer Faither says he disnae want ye in the hoose. Ah'll get him tae change his mind, but it'll take me a guid while tae dae it."

" It's aw richt Maw, ah can look efter masel."
" Aye ah ken; but Son, will ye no go up the Moss the nicht?"
" Where else can ah go?"
" Ye can sleep in the Wash Hoose. Ah'll gie ye a blanket an yin o yer Faither's auld coats. Ah'll slip ye somethin for yer breakfast tae."
" Aye, aw richt, ah'll dae it."
She sighed in relief. " Come an ah'll cook ye a big dinner. Ah got some liver frae Maxwell's."
As she set about preparing dinner, she reminded him of the unpleasant necessity of returning to School again the next day. The Attendance Officer had been again, and she'd had her second warning.
" Ah'll be up before the Baillie in Court if ye're no back the morn," she emphasised," so make sure ye're there!"
"Aye Maw," he said resignedly.
The aroma of the cooking liver set up a dull ache of hunger, and he consumed a large portion of liver, onions and potatoes in double quick time.
There was a soft knock at the door.
On opening it, Agnes took a little step back in surprise.
" Rab McKay, ah thocht ye were workin a term on a ferm?"
" Ah came awa frae it," a familiar voice replied, " they were tryin tae take a pure len o me. Is Tam in?"
Tommy forestalled her reply by appearing at the door. Rab's face broke into a grin.
" Hiya Tam, are ye comin oot?"
" Aye." He turned to his Mother," ah'll maybe see ye later; if no ah'll see ye in the mornin."
" Aye Son, ah'll have yer blankets oot there waitin for ye."
Rab looked quizzically at him, but made no comment as they exited the close into Hill Street in companionable silence.
" C'mon, will we go up the Toon?" suggested Rab brightly.
" Aye, but wait a minute."
There was something different about Rab. Tommy stood still, studying him. Rab had grown taller, there was no doubt about that; a good few inches too. He'd lost weight, but Tommy had expected that after Betty's description of him. He was wearing long breiks, an old waistcoat which had belonged to his father (he was a wee man so this fitted Rab well enough), a jacket patched at one elbow and a tweed bunnet that had seen better days.

His garb reinforced the impression that he had made the transition to a kind of manhood. He was a man earning a living, and even in these short minutes together it seemed to Tommy that Rab had a much more confident air about him.

" Whit are ye lookin at? Ye'd think ah had horns!" Rab gazed at him impatiently.

" It's no anythin, ah'm juist no used tae seein ye in lang breeks."

" Is that aw? C'mon, ah want tae see the new motors in McKay and Jardines."

Having bemoaned their personal misfortunes of the recent past en route, they gazed in admiration into the showroom window of McKay and Jardines at the fit of the Toon.

Four gleaming motor cars were arrayed, looking fit to spring into noisy life at the crank of a handle.

" Haw, look at that yin. 'Riley 6-cylinder Dewvilley': juist fower hunner and ninety five pounds, yon's a stoatir!" enthused Rab.

" It's called Deauville, efter a toon in France," pointed out Tommy smugly.

" Oh aye," shrugged Rab," yon's a stupid name, whit dae they no call it somethin Scottish for?"

Without waiting for an answer he continued," Whit yin wid ye like Tam?"

Tommy pused his lip." Ah like the wee yin."

" Whit, the 9 h.p Monaco? But yon's juist £295!"

He shook his head, as if transformed briefly into a wealthy socialite looking down his nose at the cheapest car. " Ye could have any yin."

" Naw, that's the yin ah like."

" It's got a daft name an aw: Monaco. Is that like the Wishie Co? Ah've never heard o it; an whit's 9 h.p?"

" Monaco's a wee country, roon by the sudron pairt o France, an h.p stauns for horse power. So 9 h.p means it's as strong as nine horses."

" Whit, yon totty wee thing? Awa wi ye! It's no hauf the size o yin horse! Ah'm tellin ye, yin o the muckle ploughin stallions at McLeish's Ferm wis aboot three times bigger!"

He paused, looking pensive. " Mind you," he remarked after a moment," ah heard auld McLeish havin a crack wi the Grieve, an he wis sayin that maybe next year he wis gaun tae buy a tractor tae dae the work o the horses. An ah juist got tae wonderin whit wis gaun tae happen tae thae bonnie beasts. Will he sell them tae the Knackers?"

Tommy shrugged, " Maybe he'll flog them tae another fermer."

" There cannae be many fermers lookin for horses noo; there's ower many buyin tractors. Even in the toons the motor lorries an motor charabangs are takin ower frae them."

Though Rab's knowledge of Geography and foreign tongues was scanty, he was in many ways very astute.

" Anywey," he continued, " ah got tae thinkin that when the tractor comes the Fermer'll hae nae need for hands tae work wi the horses or cutters tae bring in the harvest. By God, it wisnae much o a job as a haflin, but it peyed money, an ah'm wonderin how many fermworkers'll get jobs in a few years time; It'll no be many. An aw because o tractors and other machines!" he ended on a note of bitterness.

Tommy stared at his chum, surprised at his vehemence.

" Aye ah think yer right there," he agreed, rather lamely.

As if to confound his argument, Rab suddenly transferred his attention to the swankiest car in the display.

" Haw, lookit that yin, the Brooklands, ah widnae mind a hurl in yon, eh?" Once more he was bewitched by the seductive lure of the machine.

Tommy made a perfunctory noise of admiration. He referred Rab back to the question of jobs.

" Anywey, ah ken whit ah'm daein."

" Oh aye, whit's that then?"

" Ah'm gaun tae be a sodjer like ma Da!" he stuck out his chest in pride.

Rab looked sceptical.

" Yer ower young."

" Ah can jine the Yeomanry when ah'm sixteen."

" Aye, but yer no even fourteen yet."

Tommy was irritated that Rab had so easily wormed out the weakness in his grand design.

" Well then, whit are you gaun tae dae, big mooth?" he retorted.

" Ma Da says he kens a fermer doon by Crossford that's lookin for boys, an he's gaun tae talk tae him afore the next Feein Mercat. He says he'll get me in nae bother."

Tommy looked envious.

" See you, yer deid jammy, ah could be daein wi a joab that gets me awa frae the hoose tae ah'm auld enough tae jine up."

Rab cocked his head, brows deep in thought
" Ma Da said that the fermer wis lookin for mair than yin boy, maybe he could get you taen on as weel."
" Whit? Wid he dae that for me?"
" Aye, course he wid; ye kin he disnae get on wi yer stepfaither, so he'd be helpin ye stey oot his wey. Aye, ah'll speak tae him!"
" But mind noo," he added with a grin, " Ye'd be the halflin!"

CHAPTER 7

The school gate offered no resistance as Tommy pushed it open. No sign of anyone in the playground. That was not surprising. He knew it was early, though he did not know just how early.
In spite of her promise, his Mother had not appeared with his breakfast, though he conceded that he might have left the Wash House before she appeared. He didn't feel hungry anyhow. No wonder. What a night he'd had.
Red-eyed with lack of sleep, he shambled to the Boys' Playground, hesitating briefly as he passed by the Heidie's window. He felt a brief qualm at the inevitable thrashing which awaited him. He closed his eyes tightly, attempting to blot it out from his mind, but only succeeded in plunging himself back into the fear, confusion and unreality of the previous night.
And yet, cosy under the blankets and old overcoat, he'd nodded off to sleep in a buoyant mood, exhilarated at the possibility of joining Rab in employment. And then, after the first rush of sleep, had come the dreams.
A torrent of wordless whispers hissed in his ears. He wafted along on their tide. The voices deepened, coalescing into a vast subterranean summons.
A douche of dazzling light and he was by the great boulder on the Moss, the voice, quieter now, prickling at him. Golem-like, his legs precipitated him towards an old peat bank.
A pair of eyes tore at him through the night, coming at him with a roar. A sudden icy wind plucked at him and threw him from their path. The beast squealed in rage as he was snatched from its jaws.
He hit the ground hard. A voice cursed near at hand. There was blood in his mouth. He spat and rolled over. The impatient rattle of a car, its headlights drowning the street in a glarey pool.
A tweed-coated man glowered down at him.
" Are ye daft boy, staunin in the middle o the road as if ye were wannert? Ah ver near kilt ye!" he raved, half in shock, half in anger.
Tommy stared wide eyed, unable to grasp the reality of the situation.
" Are ye aw right son?" the driver asked urgently.

Tommy nodded and picked himself up, not looking the man in the eye, but scanning his surroundings right to left.

The man edged back to his car, muttering," The boy's a Daftie," to an unseen passenger.

" Well watch where yer gaun in future!"

The door slammed and the car drew off, the gas lit night pursuing it until it turned into Main Street.

He was in Hill Street! Wide awake and alone in the frosty desolation of night. How had he got here?

The sweat trickled down his back in rivulets of icy fear. He grogged out more blood. His tongue was numb; he must have bitten it in the fall.

A wild gust of wind had precipitated him away out of the path of the car, but now the frost hung in the air: there was not a breath of wind.

A whisper, soft as a feather.

He fled down the hill, tearing into the Close, a thousand bogles scraiching at his tail.

He shouldered the Wash House door shut and wedged his back against it, peching in the chill air. A gust huffed against it; then only silence.

Wearit and dumfoonert, he made to burrow under the blankets. His heart louped, startled by the sight of the curled up figure already there.

He looked down at himself, fast asleep in the gloom. He screwed his eyes tight shut, wishing it away.

He awoke with a start. a wild eyed boy peered down at him for an instant, then winked out of existence; the last remnant of the dream.

There was blood in his mouth. He must've had a horrifying nightmare and bitten his tongue in terror. He spat against the wall.

A sudden icy draught channelled under the door. He started and sat up. A clot of darkness grew in the far corner of the Wash House, from it emanating the faint echo of a call. The darkness blotted out the corner. An insubstantial form clawed at it, trying to scrabble out, then the wind cried 'Whisht' under the door, and the corner was as before.

Tommy at that point had donned the coat, swathed himself in the blankets and propped himself against the wall, a brick at his side.

He had not shut an eye until the Leerie Man appeared as grey dawn oozed out of the lift. Then he'd had a short doze, but fearful of a recurrence of the dreams, he'd jerked awake after a very short time.

And now, here he was, having tarried no longer in vain attempts at sleep.

The morning was chill and dank. During the night a great bundle of cloud had halted a developing frost, but its rawness remained. His new jersey, warmer though it was, could not keep it at bay.

He daunnered round the playground, trying to make sense of his eerie thoughts. He was by nature a deep, reserved boy. He'd learned to keep his feelings to himself mostly, though he possessed a volcanic temper which burst to the surface under provocation. But often he'd be seen in deep concentration, completely oblivious of his surroundings and of anyone but himself.

In just such a reverie, his feet propelled him round a circuit of the playground, questing to order his confused thoughts. Why was he experiencing these disturbing dreams?

Eventually there came realisation that something was cutting through the clamour of the past few days: something distinct from the tangle of his domestic and social relationships. Some inexplicable force, within or outwith himself, was trying to draw him. Even now he felt a momentary desire to head off at a tangent through the school gate.

He crushed the impulse savagely.

" Yer juist feart o Auld Ridnose's tawse!" he told himself.

A distant siren wailed despairingly, snapping him out of his bout of introspection. He looked around.

The Janitor, who was also the Attendance Officer, had just opened the school gates and was peering over in his direction. Tommy thought he could detect a look of malevolent satisfaction on the auld bugger's face.

A younger girl slouched through the gates and made her way to the Girls' Playground.

" Must be aboot hauf eight, it'll no be ower lang noo," he mused as he observed small knots of pupils descending the Station Steps or making their way along Alexander Street. Reluctant to face the sneers of his classmates, he retreated to the Wet Weather Shelter and huddled in a corner.

Soon the open spaces throbbed with yells and catcalls. Near at hand a group of lads kicked a chuckie around with all the concentration of Cup Final footballers. He could hear the strains of a peever rhyme emanating from the Girls' Playground. A younger boy duked and dodged his way through the shelter, hotly pursued by another laddie trying to tig him.

Though he was aware of his imminent appointment with the Headmaster, he sighed with relief as the jangling tones of the bell were scattered abroad.

The Janitor, puffed up with his own importance, whirled the bell above his head like a mad Dervish brandishing a scimitar.

" C'mon, stop yer gemmes an get tae yer lines!" he bellowed to the rapt footballers. Completely oblivious, they played on. One of them welted the chuckie and it skited through the goal.

" Goal! That's twa wan tae the 'Well!" cheered the scorer.

" Naw, it wisnae in, it wis ower the post. It's still wan each!" disputed the goalie, red faced and indignant.

" Whit! Open yer een, it wis in!" piled in a team mate of the scorer.

Another bellow from the Janitor at last caught their attention.

" Come on, the gemme's a bogey," shrilled the goalie.

As they fled towards the almost formed lines, Tommy heard him add opportunistically, " Rangers wan, Motherwell wan; the replay's at playtime." The scorer gave him a playful kick up the erse.

Tommy keeked out round the edge of the shelter. Judging his moment, he sprinted to join the end of his line, and arrived just as the doors were thrown open.

A gowned figure swept through and perched at the top of the steps, hands on hips. It was Auld Broon, known as the Heid Bummer, the Head of Maths. Without a word, he waited for absolute silence.

There was a muffled exclamation of pain in an adjoining line. The goalie in the football match had just elbowed the boy behind him in the stomach. Tommy saw that the victim was his erstwhile opponent. The victim returned the compliment with a sly dig in the ribs.

Tommy glanced at the Heid Bummer to see if he'd noticed, aware from past experience that even minor Lines infractions were unlikely to escape his gaze. Indeed he was already pointing in the direction of the miscreants. He waggled his finger. Crestfallen, they shambled up the steps. The wordless tableau continued. The Heid Bummer jerked his thumb over his shoulder in the direction of his room.

Tommy's classmates finally twigged to his presence only as they entered the Registration Room. Tommy, as usual, took a seat on his own at the front of the class.

" Haw, look who comes; Smelly Nellie!" A tall, beefy lad named Tosh Nisbet pointed him out to his cronies who were invariably clustered at the back of the class, as far out of the Maister's way as possible.

Tommy glared in the general direction of the back of the class.

" Who's gaun tae get catch it frae Auld Ridnose for plunkin it!" chortled a small, sleekit looking lad with buck teeth and a mop of spiky fair hair. He was known to all and sundry as Rabbit Heid, and as if to divert attention from his own unfortunate appearance, he had the sharpest tongue in the class, and took great delight in the misfortunes of others.
" Shut yer gub, ye wee nyaff!" snapped Tommy.
" Dinnae talk tae ma wee pal like that!"
Carrot Heid smirked provocatively. Rabbit Heid and Carrot Heid were an unlikely twosome, but were inseparable partners in playground trouble: Rabbit Heid supplying the cunning and Carrot Heid the brawn.
Carrot Heid, now more confident with his classmates to back him up, pointed a fat finger at Tommy.
" Anywey, ah've got a bone tae pick wi you, ye wee keech. Ah'm gaun tae make mincemeat oot o ye efter Auld Ridnose is feenished wi ye!" he threatened.
In the midst of more complex troubles, this dispute with Carrot Heid seemed of little consequence to Tommy. He tutted, then eyed him coldly, " Aye, yer ower feart tae gie me a square go when ye're yersel."
" Aye, he never fechts wi anybody withoot his pals," affirmed Netty McLeish, who was no lover of Carrot Heid and his cronies.
Tommy flashed her a smile of gratitude.
This blow to Carrot Heid's status was more than he could bear. He flushed red as a beetroot and made to come at Tommy down the passageway.
" Teacher!" shrilled the girl sitting nearest the door. Approaching footfalls confirmed the fact.
" You're for it!" growled Carrot Heid and lumbered back to his seat.
' Faither' McMillan, the Registration Teacher strode in, appraising the class at a glance. He halted half way across the floor, aware of the tension in the room. Though his classes were usually orderly when he entered, this was too quiet, an ominous silence. He sniffed the air for trouble like a wily auld bloodhound. He was not a bad sort, but no soft touch; a firm but fair disciplinarian. His eyes rested on Tommy.
" Ah Neill, the Prodigal returns."
" Yes Sir." Tommy's head went down.
" I do believe the Headmaster will wish to speak to you laddie, and I don't believe he'll kill the Fatted calf."
The allusion was lost on most of the class, but a few girls giggled half heartedly.

"Right, off you go!"

Tommy slunk out of the door, crossed the Hall and knocked faintly at the Headmaster's door. There was no answer. He knocked more firmly. An irritable 'Come In!'

"Tommy Neill, Sir. Mr McMillan sent me."

The tall, gowned figure ignored him and continued to stare out at the empty playground. A yatter of black headed gulls careered overhead, their falsetto rending the silence.

Tommy cleared his throat, anxious to get the punishment over with.

The chug of a passing motor van. Hard edged silence within the room.

"Mr McMillan sent me, Sir," he repeated.

"Neill, before I belt you, as I inevitably shall, I wish you to answer one small question," the Headmaster responded unexpectedly, still peering out of the window.

Another silence oozed out of the walls, broken only by the crack of fresh coal in his well kennelled fire.

"What is it Sir?" prompted Tommy.

"Why?"

Tommy wrinkled his features, "Whit d'ye mean Sir?"

"I mean why do you persist in playing truant!" The voice lashed at him as Mr Redpath whirled round. His eyes, magnified by thick spectacles, attacked him.

Tommy tottered back a step.

"Why?" The voice soft again.

"Ah'm no shair, Sir," Tommy stuttered.

The Headmaster arched his eyebrows.

"I'm not really sure, Sir," Tommy recovered himself.

Mr Redpath regarded him appraisingly.

"Neill, you are one of the brightest pupils in the school, I know that you excel in most subjects. Your teachers tell me that you take a keen interest in your work."

He paused, scanning Tommy's features for a flicker of reaction.

"I wish to know, I don't have to know; I shall belt you regardless, but I wish to know."

Somewhat nonplussed at the openness with which the Headmaster was speaking, Tommy's thoughts swam momentarily. He made to speak a glib lie, then changed his mind: perhaps frankness deserved frankness.

" Hauf the boys in ma class are aye cawin me doon Sir. Ah get fair scunnered wi it. It's no that ah dinnae care aboot the lessons Sir."
Ignoring the use of the Vernacular, the Headmaster nodded, as if this confirmed his private thoughts.
" You've got to face your problems boy. It's no use always trying to run away from them."
" Ah usually dae, Sir, but it fair gets ye doon sometimes."
There seemed to be the ghost of a twinkle in the Headmaster's eye, then his expression hardened, and he opened his drawer.
" And now if you don't mind raising your hands."
He withdrew a two thonged tawse, shiny with frequent use.
Flummoxed by the sudden change in mood, Tommy quivered as he outstretched his arms and crossed his hands. He delved into the recesses of his mind to screen out the oncoming pain.
The tawse arced towards him. A crack of pain raced up his arm. He changed hands automatically, shutting out the pain, retreating within himself into a sudden pit of blackness.
An eon of dark as only the dead know. Season slow churning of the earth around as the worms and maggots tunneled and laid and munched into the dust that had once been him. Soil pressing into the cavities left by his decaying flesh. Bones like roots trying in vain to grow a new man. Earth stirring at the Sun's kiss, but no light pierces the eternal dark.
It was at times like this that one hated the implementation of Rules thought the Headmaster. Rules were essential of course for the Greater Good of Society; but still, when dealing with a boy like Neill, it was a pity that the rules could not be more flexible.
He looked down at Tommy. Eyes screwed firmly shut, the lad had erected a wall against the pain. The life seemed to have fled from him, or retreated deep within, as in hibernation. The inner strength of the boy disconcerted him. What a waste. It galled him that the boy's talent would be unnurtured by Higher Education. It would no doubt evaporate under the onslaught of social and economic deprivation. He'd seen it all before. So many had slipped through his fingers.
As he wound up for the second stroke, he suddenly cried out as the tawse seemed to take on a life of its own. It flew out of his hand as if repelled by a fierce magnetic surge. A wave of cold raged round the room, knocking the breadth from him and sending his senses shrieking. His legs crumpled

beneath him, momentarily transformed into quivering boneless strips of flesh. He clung to his desk as a drowning man clings to flotsam amidst the maelstrom.

There was somebody else on the room; of that he was sure. Venomous eyes played over him. He looked round wildly. No one had entered. there was no one else there save for Neill, who, astonishingly, still stood arms upraised, as if in a trance.

A hard knot of power seemed to radiate in the room. Was that a shadow by the fire?

Then there was nothing save the waxing and waning of the flames. Their merry dance held him, and the presence departed, evaporated like mist under the breath of the Sun.

By God, he was getting too old for this job he thought. Imagining things, and losing control like this; and in front of a pupil too. It would be round the whole school. Auld Ridnose (for he was well aware of his nickname) had taken a mad turn, either that or they'd say he'd been fou.

And yet.... he could have sworn there was someone else in the room. He'd never experienced anything like that before. Obviously some kind of weird mental attack. Nerves getting the better of him. The sweat prickled his forehead. He removed his glasses and rubbed his eyes. He'd need to see his doctor.

He looked at Neill and shivered. He looked mesmerised, totally unaware of his surroundings. What was the matter with him? Perhaps he had caused all this. Was it some sort of fit?

If it was, perhaps his own unaccountable behaviour had not been witnessed by Neill.

" Neill, snap out of it Boy!"

Rough hands pummelled him.

" Neill, what's the matter with you, laddie?"

The light blazed all around. Who had awakened him from his eternity of slumber?

" Are you all right, boy?"

Tommy grimaced as a glowing patch of light snaked under his eyelids. He flickered open his eyes, absorbing short flashes of reality.

A dark, cowled man, framed in a halo of light, loomed over him.

Was his long hiatus in Purgatory finally ended?

Then the light softened, dividing itself into Shadow and Light.

The Headmaster spoke urgently in his ear.
Tommy's dark Odyssey had ended. He regarded the Headmaster squarely. The Headmaster's shoulders relaxed. Clearly, Neill was with him once more. Odd, it was as if his very spirit had fled, leaving only a shell, and was now returned to inhabit the body. He shivered once more, sending uncontrolled ripples dancing down his gown. Icy gobs of sweat rivulated down his back. Why was he thinking such outlandish thoughts?
" Are you all right?" he mumbled.
" Yes, Sir."
The pain had departed from Tommy's hand. Had he imagined the belting? What a notion he'd just had. Blotting out the tawse, he'd imagined himself underground. It had been so vivid, not like the wispy reality of a dream. It was as if he'd been buried; he'd even smelt the tang of the earth. He wrunkled his nose.
A corpse.
Yes, that was what it had felt like. His eyes rolled. A corpse in the glitty earth. The things that went on inside your head. Still it seemed to have kept the pain at bay.
The Heidie looked down at him with panic stricken eyes. He looked as jittery as a nervy cuddy.
He was beginning to regain control of himself, but still regarded Tommy warily.
" He thinks ah'm awa wi the fairies." The thought played in Tommy's mind.
" Are you sure you're all right?"
" Ah'm fine, Sir; whit wey should ah no be?" replied Tommy spiritedly, puzzled by the extent of the Headmaster's concern.
" It was just that..... oh never mind. Off you go."
Tommy stole a quick glance at him as he closed the Office door. For the first time ever Auld Ridnose did not seem fully in control.
" It's like he's feart o me," mused Tommy. He rejected the notion immediately.
" Maybe the man's no weel the day," he concluded.
He eyed the clock in the Hall. Nine forty five. Half an hour had passed. He could have sworn he'd been in the Heidie's Office for only a few minutes. He rubbed his eyes. It was lack of sleep that was playing these tricks on him. Funny how it seemed to make you lose your grip on reality.
Registration was over. It was well into the first period of the day: Maths with the Heid Bummer. The prospect did not fill him with enthusiasm. However,

as far as anyone knew, he was still being interviewed by the Headmaster. On an impulse, he stole along the corridor and out of the Boys' Door to the toilets. Perhaps he could catch up on some of his lost sleep. He wrunkled up his nose as he entered the outside Toilet Block. Though freshly disinfected by the Janitor each morning, the toilets still stank of stale piss.

He entered one of the shabby cubicles, bolted the door behind him, and sat down on the seat, having automatically checked it for skelfs before he did so. Not very comfortable. He slid off the seat and cooried into the corner.

A draught puffed under the door and rocked it gently on its hinges. He curled himself up. The draught plucked at his hair.

A sea of fresh air around. Hot sun on his back. The Wind had whisked him here, its tide rippling over the long grass. The great Boulder slumbered. The Earth birled around it.

Night, Day, Shadow, Rain, Sun, Frost, Snow: nothing could awaken this dark sleeper hunched against the World.

Voices.

Echoes scaling the fortress of his sleep.

A heavy body falling.

A dull blow to the front of his head. The back of his skull cracked sickeningly against the wall.

Geordie had caught up with him at last.

Instinctively he covered his head with his arms. Hot blood from the back of his head dripped through his fingers. he waited for the blows.

" Yer richt where ye belang, ye wee shite, a tollie on the flair o the shunkie. Thought ye could hide frae me, did ye?"

The voice was Carrot Heid's not Geordie's. Tommy started and dropped his arms. Carrot Heid leered down at him, his bulk filling the cubicle. Above his shoulder a gargoyle cackled: Rabbit Heid, smirking over the partition of the next cubicle.

" We've got ye noo!" Rabbit heid snickered. " See, ah tellt ye he'd be in here!" he crowed to his crony.

Tommy began to get his wits about him. The door was bolted. Obviously Carrot Heid had louped over the partition from the next cubicle. He was trapped like a rat in the corner.

But a cornered rat could still give a good account of itself. Covering his head with both arms he attempted to rise awkwardly, but a savage kick in the shin poleaxed him. He sobbed in frustration.

" That's it big fella, gie him laldy!" chortled Rabbit Heid.
Calmly Carrot Heid waited for the next move.
Tommy groaned in pain, then regaining a measure of control, he groaned again somewhat theatrically, feigning more serious injury.
" Haw, maybe ye've broke his leg." Rabbit Heid's voice adopted a note of concern. Tommy groaned again. Out of the corner of his eye he observed that Carrot Heid seemed to have been taken in somewhat. The cocky expression had vanished, perhaps there was a hint of guilt. He peered down at Tommy, who still lay in a crumpled heap.
This was the chance Tommy had been waiting for. Bracing both palms, he propelled himself upwards. Carrot Heid grunted in surprise, but still managed to skite Tommy a glancing blow which caught him on the lip.
But now Tommy stood triumphantly on his feet. The raw taste of fresh blood inflamed his fury, and with an animal snarl he charged at the bigger boy, butting him full in the face.
Carrot Heid's heavy body catapulted against the locked door. The bolt shot loose and the door clattered open. Carrot Heid tumbled hard down on his erse, the force of the fall sending him head over heels. He lay stunned, his nose spurting blood.
Tommy swaggered towards him. Carrot Heid cringed and covered his head with his arms.
" Naw, ah'll no hit ye when ye're doon, ye muckle yella-belly bastard; no like ye did tae me!"
He placed the sole of his boot on top of the well protected head, much like a hunter in a victorious pose over a kill.
" Mind yer mooth," he growled, " next time ah'll no be sae saft wi ye!"
Carrot Heid quivered, but made no reply.
Tommy became aware of the din of playground noises outside. A smaller boy, framed in the toilet entrance, gaped open mouthed at the tableau within. Tommy glared at him and he fled.
" Haw youse, there's been a big fight in the Boys' Toilets. Smelly Nellie's got big Carrot Heid doon on the grun; he's hauf killed him!" The voice shrilled across the yard.
A faint sound emerged from the neighbouring cubicle.
Tommy wheiched round and kicked the half open door against the wall.
" Aye an as for you, ye slevery wee nyaff," he spat at the deathly pale figure of Rabbit Heid, prostrated against the back wall of the cubicle, " ah'm gaun

tae mollocate ye!"
The clanging tones of the bell to end the Morning Interval.
"We'll be late for the Lines!" blurted out Rabbit Heid. Tommy made no reply. A faint smirk dogged his lips.
" C'mon Tam, we'll catch it frae the Heid Bummer."
Rabbit Heid, ever the fly man, seemed eminently reasonable.
" Tryin tae sook in, ye wee bastard, are ye? Anywey, ye're wrang- we're no gaun tae catch it, you are!"
He darted forward and caught Rabbit Heid by the scruff of the neck. With a swift movement, Tommy thrust his head down the toilet pan and held it under, then hauled him out. Swiftly he slammed the door of the cubicle, leaving the sploonging figure boaking on the toilet floor.
Jumping over the still prostrate figure of Carrot Heid, he skelped out of the toilet towards the now formed Lines, chortling with glee.
Half the eyes in the school seemed to be observing him as he took his place at the end of his line. He cut a wild figure, his hair matted with dried blood, a thin trickle of blood channelling from his cut lip, clothes dishevelled, and a fiercely victorious air. He ignored the stares of those around and breathed in the fresh air. He looked about him.
The dank, mucky sky was clearing. The cloud had been ripped off neatly, and a great blue rent was advancing from the north. The colder, drier air had already made inroads into the damp lethargy of the early part of the morning. Tommy sucked it into his lungs. One of his personal clouds seemed to have been dispelled for the moment.
Out of the corner of his eye, he noted that the Heid Bummer had appeared, and that the first of the lines were filing in silently. He peered suspiciously back at the Toilet Block. His two adversaries had not made their appearance; obviously lying low whilst the lines were going in. He'd sort them out!
A craw alighted silently on the nearby roof. It cocked its head and seemed to peer straight down at him with strange empty eyes. Tommy glowered back. Its een, dowie and fathomless, seemed to draw him momentarily. Then, with an abrupt ' Keeaw', it clawed itself into the air.
Tommy's line was last, and as he approached the Heid Bummer, he halted.
" Sir, there's two boys still in the Toilets, they've been fighting."
The Heid Bummer looked down at the dried gore on Tommy's scalp. " Are you sure you weren't involved in this fight?"
" No Sir, I fell and dunted my head earlier."

" All right, in you go!"
Tommy smirked as the Heid Bummer set off with a determined stride towards the Toilets. His revenge seemed to be complete.
Miss Campbell, the English Teacher, started as he made his way into her classroom.
" Tommy, come here this instant!" she said, with obvious concern.
A pretty, stylish woman in her Thirties with perfectly waved auburn hair, she stood not much taller than Tommy.
She scanned the top of his head with a worried frown.
" How on earth did you come by such a dreadful cut?"
" I fell, Miss."
She cocked her head and adopted a sceptical expression.
" I was fighting, Miss," he admitted. He had never been able to lie to Miss Campbell, whose treatment of him was markedly more sympathetic and encouraging than any other teacher in the school.
" I thought so. Well, you're in luck. That needs treatment, and it just so happens that the School Nurse is here this morning. Right, get yourself along to the Medical Room. Tell her I sent you."
The Nurse humphed as Tommy winced in pain at the sting of the spirit on his wound.
" This is rather a bad cut you know. What's this?" She caught her breath abruptly. Roughly, she inspected his scalp.
She stood back and regarded him accusingly.
" You're excluded from School for the rest of the week!"
He blinked, "What for? It's only a wee scratch!"
" It's nothing to do with your cut. Your head is alive with nits. There's no excuse for that in a boy of your age.!"
Tommy thought of the night spent in Hairy Wullie's hut.
" What do I do now?"
" You go straight home. I'll inform the School. You'd best get that crop of hair shorn off as soon as possible. I'll give you a special shampoo. Wash your scalp thoroughly over several days and that should do the trick.
She handed him a thick envelope.
" Right, off home; and don't come back until next Monday!" she said briskly.

CHAPTER 8

Tommy knocked faintly at the McKay's door. There was a chatter of female conversation within. The door opened and Lizzie McKay peered through her spectacles at the figure confronting her. Her neighbour Bessie Chalmers stared curiously from within.

" Is Rab in, Mrs McKay?" asked Tommy respectfully.

" Aw it's you Tommy, ah ver near didnae ken ye under thon bunnet. Are ye no at the Schule?"

" Naw Mrs McKay, ah'm excluded," he mumbled.

Lizzie regarded him with momentary distaste, but this gave way to a more sympathetic expression. She remembered his original question.

" Oor Robert's no in, he's awa tae the Mercat wi his Faither, he'll likely no be back till fower.."

Tommy's face fell.

" Ah weel, ah'll probably see him then. Cheerio."

He shuffled off down the Close.

Lizzie and Bessie watched him go.

Bessie shook her head, " It's a pure sin for that laddie, he's aye that puirhoose lookin."

" Aye, so it is," Lizzie agreed.

" Aye an that Mother o his swankin aboot the place, wearin nothin but the best, or so she'd have ye believe," Bessie snorted.

" Aye, and as for that courss brute o a man, aye leatherin the boy. Oor Betty was sayin that he flung the laddie oot the other nicht an noo he's sleepin ootside," Lizzie said indignantly.

" Well ah never, terrible so it is!" Bessie was scandalised.

Lizzie watched as the pathetic figure with the too large bunnet disappeared through the Close.

" Aye, naebody looks efter him, he's juist a lost sowl, nothin but a lost sowl."

CHAPTER 9

After lying low until his Stepfather had departed for work, he'd returned home.
His Mother had sent him immediately up to Tory Young the barber, who'd had him shorn in minutes flat.
Now, as he gazed into the window of Ikey Moses's shop, his scalp tingled with the carbolic shampoo. He hid his bare head under one of his Stepfather's old bunnets, which threatened to fall off at the first gust of wind and so reveal his shame to all and sundry.
His Mother had given him scant sympathy, flyting on him for catching vermin; but after he'd returned from the barber's she'd made him a couple of pieces and given him a mug of hot tea.
Miserable and cold, as he looked in the window he felt that his world was dissolving around him, but there, at the heart of the strangeness, was the Moss and the call of the thing that dwelt there. He no longer doubted it. Some dark fate was beckoning him. Events of the past few days seemed to have been shaped for that purpose. But who or what was the shaper?
A feeling of being watched had saved him from drowning. A frightening day-dream had spared him the pain of the tawse. Nothing had saved him from the injuries inflicted by Carrot Heid, but then without them he'd never have been excluded. The idea dawned that this exclusion was the latest in a line of not necessarily benevolent events. He now believed that they were purely to serve the purpose of the Shaper.
Immediately he rejected the intuition. How could that be? He was getting fair wannert again. Even so, for an instant he cleared his mind and concentrated.
Emptiness. No wild entreaties or questing from without.
No doubt he'd end up at the Moss again soon, but today was not that day. His Mother had blamed Hairy Wullie and indirectly the Moss for his infestation. She'd warned him within an inch of his life against going there again.
Well for today he'd happily use that as an excuse he decided. Besides it was

too late, and he was meeting Rab later.
The kaleidoscope of Soor Plooms, Stripit Balls, Beveridge, Lucky Tatties and bars of Five Boys refocused in his eyes. His mouth watered but, as usual, he hadn't a brass farthing. He looked into the shop. The skinny figure of Ikey peered out at him curiously. Ikey darted a glance at the back shop, then furtively beckoned Tommy in.
Puzzled, Tommy entered. The bell on the door jangled noisily. Ikey jumped, and looked guiltily through the back. All seemed quiet. He glanced back at Tommy and put his finger to his lips. Deftly he emptied a goodly number of Stripit Balls, at least half a pound in weight, into a poke, and practically in the same movement, thrust them into Tommy's hands.
Astonishment spread over Tommy's features. Ikey inclined his head towards the door and once more put his finger over his lips.
" Thanks Mr Fraser," Tommy whispered, and made to exit.
The doorbell jangled, and a harsh voice halted him in his tracks.
" Ah hope ye've peyed for them!"
A muckle red-faced woman, built like a heifer, framed the doorway.
" Eh aye, Mrs Fraser," Tommy stuttered.
" Ye liar, ah wis watchin frae ootside!" she bowfed, advancing threateningly.
" Ah wis gaun tae pey for them the morn," Tommy altered his line.
Her expression darkened into a thunderplump of fury. Behind the counter, Ikey quailed.
" Ah tellt ye, nae tick!" She clumped over to the counter and clouted Ikey a dull one on the lug.
" They'll be nae tick in this shop!" she spat, and rattled him again. He cringed like a chastened schoolboy.
She breinged round to the other side of the counter.
" Ye're naethin but a useless wee whitterick!"
She grabbed his collar, and whummled him like a ragdoll.
Tommy looked on, an incredulous spectator. Never had he witnessed such bullying.
" Leave him alane Missus!" he protested, shocked at the treatment of the wee man.
She drew him a look that would have turned milk sour, but did at least stop shaking her man.
" Get oot o this shop afore ah clip yer ear, ye wee tink! Aye an pit doon yon poke o sweeties; ye havenae peyed for them!"

" Stick them up yer erse!" Tommy flung the sweets across the shop at her. Without flinching at the skittering cascade of stripit balls that ricocheted around her, she louped with all her huge bulk over the counter. But Tommy was too quick for her. He duked through the door and pelted off in the direction of the Station Steps.

She bellowed after him, " Ah'll caw the lugs aff ye when ah get a haud o ye! An dinnae come back tae this shop again either!"

Tommy turned, made a face, and waggled his fingers in his ears, but the gesture was lost on her, as she was already re-entering the shop. The door slammed and almost jumped from its hinges.

Concerned at the fate of Ikey, Tommy crept back along the street, secure in the knowledge that he could outrun the auld battleaxe should she give chase.

Margaret Williams, who lived beside the Close mouth, had been an interested spectator of the last scenario. She was a bit of a gossip, though in no way a malicious woman. She hovered by the shop curiously, sensing a choice tit bit for her next blether with her cronies. Her eyebrows arched questioningly as he approached.

Tommy still could not get over the events he had so recently witnessed.

" She was hittin him. Ah tried tae stop her," he blurted out.

" Is she back at that again?" Margaret nodded knowingly.

" D'ye ken aboot it?" Tommy was surprised.

" Aye, it'll no be the first time, an it'll no be the last. No the least bit nice yon wummin. Thinks she's a cut above us aw. But it wis his money that bought the shop. An she's juist the same as the rest o us; Lexie twa stairs up wis at the Schule wi her. Aye, her faither wis a courss brute o a man. She's got a lot o him in her. An ignorant wummin, ah dinnae ken whit he saw in her, though ah've heard speak that she tellt him she wis....." Propriety halted her flow of revelations.

" Whit?" Tommy wanted to know.

" Naw son, ye're ower young tae ken aboot thae kind o things. Anywey, ah feel heart sorry for that man o hers!"

Tommy nodded his agreement and she made off up Hill Street. He sneaked up to the shop window and peered in surreptitiously. Ikey was alone, dispiritedly tidying up the counter. An angry weal stood out on his cheek. He looked like a crushed flower. Something made him look up. His eyes met Tommy's; all the cares of the World dwelt there. For an instant an eerie feeling of kinship stirred in Tommy's mind. Then Ikey dropped his gaze and scurried through to the back shop.

Tommy decided to make his way to the Mercat to see if he could find Rab. As he turned into Caley Road though, he observed the unmistakeable figure of Frank McKay, with Rab in attendance, making their way down the brae. He rushed up to them enthusiastically.

Frank eyed him up and down, a twinkle in his eye.

" Aw aye, Chief Sittin Bull on the warpath again is he?"

Tommy blinked, nonplussed.

" Whit Mr McKay?"

" Ye've been scalped Son!"

"Aw aye." Tommy cooried under his bunnet.

" Guess whit's in the box!" Rab smirked, indicating the cardboard box under his Father's arm. Something scrabbled inside.

Rab's Mother was always demented with the exotic and unexpected things which Frank was liable to bring home from Mercat.

"A rabbit?" he hazarded.

" Naw. Take a peek an find oot." Frank laughed in anticipation.

Caunnily, Tommy eased open the lid. Instantly something snapped at his fingers. Startled, he drew back. With an indignant quack, the long neck of an angry white duck was thrust out of the box. It glowered from side to side.

" Whit are ye gaun tae dae wi it?" asked Tommy in amazement, as Frank closed the lid none too gently.

" That's the morn's dinner ye gowk!" laughed Rab.

" Anywey Son, ah've got news for ye," Frank continued as they strolled past Thornlie Kirk, " Juist by luck we came on Tam Eadie up at the Mercat, ken the fermer frae by Crossford that Oor Rab wis tellin ye aboot.. He's lookin tae tak on twa boys, he wis let doon by the last boys. Anywey, Oor Rab's startin on Monday; we've shook haunds on it. Ah tellt him aboot ye: ah said ye were a guid steady laddie. The job's yours if ye want it, but ye'll hae tae make up yer mind by Monday. Tam's aw richt, he disnae pey weel, but he looks efter his boys."

Tommy positively jigged in exhilaration.

Rab caught his father's eye and winked.

" That wis awfu guid o ye, Mr McKay!" Tommy blurted out.

" That's aw richt, but dinnae let me doon, or I'll boot yer erse!" Frank growled, mock seriously.

62

" Ah wouldnae dae such a thing!" Tommy was shocked.
" So ah'll tell Auld Eadie ye'll be startin a week on Monday as ma halflin.!" guffawed Rab.
Tommy gave him a playful clout, and they capered about the pavement, feinting and ducking.
" Richt, stop yer wrasslin!"
Frank caught Tommy by the scruff of the neck. He looked into his eyes, all laughter wrung from his face.
" Ye're sure aboot the job? It's sair toil."
" Aye Mr McKay."
" Grand!" Frank nodded in satisfaction, " besides, it'll keep ye oot o the road o Bugger Lugs doon by." He inclined his head towards Smith's Land.
Tommy flashed him a smile, then turned to Rab.
" C'mon," he enthused, "we'll gang up the Toon!"
Rab regarded his father, " Is that aw richt Da?"
" Aye, on ye go, but be back in time for yer tea."
Tommy keeked into the Smiddy as they passed. A great Clydesdale, high as half a hillock, was in the process of being shod. He wondered what it was like to work with them.
" They're bonnie douce beasts. Ye'll be fair taen on wi them: that's if the fermer hasnae sellt them aw an bocht a tractor."
Rab was glum for a moment.
" C'mon," he urged after a moment's reverie, " up tae the Poly!"
Miss Leggate's Toyshop, or the Poly, to give it its more common title, was the best toyshop in Wishaw.
Particularly in their younger days, Rab and Tommy in common with quite a few of their contemporaries, had whiled away many a happy hour staring at the wonders within. This current expedition then, was something in the way of a nostalgic journey back in time to the more carefree days of the Past. However, Their journey was not to be completed.
As the chums rounded into Main Street by Victoria Buildings, a cultured voice hailed him.
Miss Campbell, smartly dressed in a coat with a fox fur, stood behind him.
" Tommy Neill?" She looked doubtfully for an instant as she scanned his ravaged scalp, which was all too obvious even under the bunnet.
" Yes Miss," mumbled Tommy.
" What on earth have you done to yourself?"

" Ah had to get all ma hair cut off Miss, ah had bugs."
" Yes, I guessed that....I....," she was nonplussed momentarily at his directness.
" And you're sleeping out of doors?" She brought up the subject she had wished to raise with him.
" How did ye ken ..., how did you know Miss?" he corrected himself automatically.
Rab shuffled awkwardly behind him.
" Ah'll away hame Tam," he announced softly.
Miss Campbell noticed him for the first time.
" I'm sorry Robert, I hope I haven't interrupted anything."
Rab blushed, " Naw Miss, it's time for ma tea the noo anyway."
" How are you getting on?"
" Fine Miss. On Monday ah start a term on a ferm down by
Crossford." Quiet pride shone in his eyes.
" I'm glad to hear that. I always thought you'd be better away from the Works and out in the Country. Best of luck. I'm sure you'll do well."
" Thanks Miss Campbell, nice tae see ye again." He blushed even more deeply, then whirled round and scurried off with a 'See ye later Tam' as he rounded the corner.
Miss Campbell's smile died and was replaced by a look of concern.
" I overheard Robert's sister talking about you, and I tackled her about it. She told me what she knew. Is it true?"
" Aye Miss."
" Just look at you, out all night wearing only a sweater and breiks."
" Ah've got some blankets," Tommy protested faintly.
" No, this won't do!" She shook her head, swithered for a moment, then announced decisively, " Right, come with me!"
She took his hand and marched him along the street.
" Ye're no taking me to the Poor Hoose?" he blurted out.
" Of course not!" she snapped.
Tommy, embarrassed at being led by the hand like a big wean walked meekly at her side. Without hesitation she led him into the Co Drapery.
Twenty minutes later they were striding along Belhaven Terrace. Tommy was laden with parcels. In a whirlwind she had purchased him a coat, long trousers, semmits, pants and a pair of boots.
" Miss, ye shouldnae have done that, spendin yer money on me, yon coat

cost near thirty shillins," he was protesting, flabbergasted at the turn of events.
" It was necessary." She gave him a glance that precluded further argument, then turned into the driveway of a smart semi detached bungalow.
" Right, in you come," she said briskly.
" But this is yer ain hoose!"
She arched her eyebrows. Tommy said no more.
She unlocked the door and showed him into the front Lounge. A good fire was well kennelled, flames licking at the grate.
" Right, put these parcels down and sit yourself down by the fire."
Tommy squatted on the hearthrug.
" Why don't you sit on the armchair?" she asked, half amused.
" Ah'm no sittin on yer guid chair wi these mawkit troosers Miss!"
" Stuff and nonsense, sit on the chair!"
He shrugged and sank into the velvety depths of the armchair.
" Right, we'll soon have you warmed up nicely. I'll fix us some tea."
As kitchen noises echoed faintly from the rear of the house, Tommy, secure in his cocoon of snoozy warmth, gazed out at the street. Belhaven Terrace was the Nob's street, where doctors, teachers, pit owners and such like toffs stayed. Most of the houses had servants and motor cars were parked in some driveways. This swanky house of Miss Campbell's was one of the smaller ones.
He drank in the opulence of the room, missing nothing. Velvet armchairs and sofa, chintzy curtains, patterned carpet from door to window, fine china in the display cabinet, a polished oak table with the figure of an Amazon Huntress on top.
Miss Campbell smiled through the doorway.
" Tea will be ready in about half an hour."
She sat down in the armchair on the other side of the fire and looked at him penetratingly.
" Tommy, I want you to stay the night here in the Guest Bedroom. I'm not having you sleeping outside in this weather."
Somehow Tommy had guessed that this was coming. He looked at her questioningly.
" Miss, why are you doing all this?"
She stared hard at him, looking right into his eyes. There was something strange in her eyes. A woman had never looked at him like that before. He

blushed, but could not take his eyes away from her.

" There are reasons......," she murmured slowly.

Tommy tore his gaze away from her lovely eyes. Funny how he'd never thought of her like that before. She had always been just a teacher, albeit an especially fair one.

There was a silence; the fire sank down in the grate and a car rolled past.

" Will you tell me the reasons?" he stammered, avoiding her gaze.

She hesitated, was about to speak then flicked a glance at the clock on the mantelpiece.

" There's just time for you to have a bath before tea." She was the schoolteacher once more.

" A bath Miss?"

" Yes, a bath, and a hairwash. I keep a supply of some special shampoo.... "

Ah've used some o that this mornin," he interrupted.

" So much the better, another shampoo should see you clear. Follow me!"

She ushered him through the hall and into the bathroom. This was the first time he had ever seen an indoor bathroom.

" Jeez oh Miss, it's fair swanky. It's as big as the back room in oor hoose."

With a smile she turned on the taps and twin jets of hot and cold spurted out merrily.

" Just turn off the taps when it's at the temperature that suits you."

Tommy stood hypnotised by the falling water. She laid out a set of his new clothes.

" Right, you've only got a short time, tea will be ready soon."

She closed the door behind her. Slowly he undressed, tossing his clothes into an untidy heap by the sink. The bath was filling up nicely. It was slightly too cold. He wanted it hotter, so he turned off the cold and watched as the level crept slowly but steadily up. Soon he was satisfied and he swiftly stripped off his underclothes. He steeled himself against the cold, but to his surprise, he found that the room was pleasantly warm. Bare naked, he luxuriated in the steamy warmth.

The door burst open.

" I forgot to give you this shampoo..." she began. Her jaw dropped as she saw his nakedness. Her glance lingered. He looked her straight in the eyes, then slowly picked up a towel and covered his middle.

" I'm sorry, I should have knocked," she stuttered. Tommy's gaze did not leave her face. She flushed bright red, then turned quickly and closed the door.

Tommy let the towel fall. He had an erection. He could see her silhouette through the opaque glass on the door. Unhurriedly he replaced the towel on the rail. He glanced once more at the door. She had gone.

Slowly he eased himself into the water. Steam wisped around him. Slowly his erection died, but the fever of it remained. His whole body tingled, every molecule of water seemed to nuzzle him. He closed his eyes and was swallowed up in a tide of sensuality.

A sudden shaft of doubt cut through. This was illusion, a waking dream. He blinked open his eyes.

The bathroom was as before. The water lapped up to his chin. He smiled and set to administering the unpleasant shampoo. Then he soaped himself with a bar of her scented soap. He rubbed the essence of her all over him. Wrinkling his nose, he rinsed away the foulness of the shampoo, then rubbed a little of the soap over his scalp to counteract it.

He pulled out the plug and watched the oily water corkscrew widdershins down the hole. He swung out of the bath and paraded boldly to the door, but there was no shadow behind it. He swathed himself in towels and dried himself vigorously, applying puffs of talcum powder liberally.

He donned his new clothes and regarded himself in the steamy mirror. It was as if he had sloughed off the skin of his former self and re-emerged in a new identity.

Tea was formal and polite, though delicious. Miss Campbell avoided his direct gaze, and somewhat to his confusion, acted as though nothing had happened, She directed him into the Lounge, where tea would be served.

Outside the sky filled with grey dusk. The wind galumphed through the pom pom lime trees in the front border by the wall. Gold interiors shone out from the houses.

The aroma of fine tea preceded her arrival. She placed the tray in front of the fire and poured from a harsh angled teapot into the china cups. A mound of Abernethy biscuits and iced cakes were arranged on the tiers of the cake stand.

" Help yourself," she smiled.

" Now I won't put the light on if you don't mind," she continued, "I do so love to sit in the firelight. I often sit here just watching the light drain from the sky. It's so peaceful. Perhaps I'm a creature of shadows."

Tommy sipped his tea, being careful not to slurp.

" The tea's lovely Miss," he said gratefully.

" Good, I'm glad you're enjoying it."
" Miss, will you tell me why you're doing all this for me?" he asked again respectfully.
She considered.
" Yes I will, but first I want you to tell me about the circumstances which led to you sleeping outdoors."
It was pitch black outside by the time he had completed his tale. He omitted little, admitting his truancy openly, but avoiding much mention of his strange thoughts about the Moss.
She had interrupted him at one point, "Why the fascination with Greenhead Moss?"
" Ah dinnae ken, Miss. Ah've aye had a kind of fascination, as ye say, but there's somethin gey queer aboot the place the noo."
Rather to his surprise, she had given a start at that, then looked into the fire with a fey distant look. Time past shimmered in the embers.
He had continued at that point. He'd felt that she'd only been half listening after that, but she had turned her head abruptly as he concluded by saying, " Ah often wish they'd never started the War, everythin would be hunky dory; ma Da would be here tae look efter us."
She leaned back in the armchair and seemed to mop her brow with her handkerchief. After a moment, he realised that she was weeping.
" What's the matter Miss?" he asked anxiously, " Have I upset you?"
She sobbed quietly, her face a red blur in the firelight.
Full of concern, Tommy knelt down at her feet. Mascara'd tears channelled down her cheeks.
" Miss, it'll be all right!" he urged; and before he knew what he was doing, he was cradling her head in his arms. She clung to him, her tears trickling down his neck. She quivered with involuntary racking sobs. Her whole being grieved. Tommy closed his eyes, willing the grief from her, quite unconscious of the swell of her body against him.
Eventually she quietened and pushed him away gently. She dabbed at her eyes.
" Are you all right?"
" Yes I'm.......quite finished. I'm sorry about this."
" Dinnae worry about it."
She sniffed and looked into the fire. " The loneliest words in all the World: 'It might have been'," she murmured. A wry smile spread over her begrutten

features.
She looked at him shamefacedly, "What an exhibition I've made of myself. Still maybe I needed that."
" Why were ye greetin Miss, if ye dinnae mind me askin?"
Tommy felt that important things, perhaps even concerning him, lay behind her sorrow.
" Yes," she said, rising, "it's time I told you some things. Come with me."
She directed him through to her bedroom and lit the electric lamp. Baffled, Tommy hung by the doorway.
" Look at the photograph on my bedside table."
A soldier and his lass. He moved closer for a more detailed look. A young lieutenant, debonair, with a neatly trimmed moustache. He gazed fondly into the eyes of his sweetheart. It was straight out of Tommy's vision of his own future military career. It was his Father.
He whirled round to face her. She regarded him sorrowfully.
" Where did ye....?" he began, then turned back to the photograph. The pretty young girl grinning at the camera was clearly recognisable as Miss Campbell.
She held forward her hand. He'd occasionally noticed the ring that sparkled there without thinking anything of it.
" He was my fiance. We were engaged to be married."
" This wis afore....?"
" Yes, before you were born."
" But the photo wis taen during the War!"
" We were Undergraduates together..."
" Whit does that mean Miss?"
" We were at University together. Of course we knew each other vaguely before."
She looked at him with a sudden fierce flash of pride.
" Your Father was a brilliant scholar of Classics and Languages Tom."
He made to interrupt, but was silenced by a gesture.
" Anyway, he enlisted not long after war broke out. It was on his first Leave that he asked me to marry him. I accepted of course."
She looked wistfully at the photograph.
" But why did he no mairry ye?"
Her features went blank. She recited like an automaton, drowning out the pain.

"The photograph was taken at the end of 1917 on his Leave before last. We quarrelled soon after. I wanted to get married then, but he wanted to wait until the War was ended."

She spun round, all defences against the years of grief once more breached.

"The Trenches changed him. He spent most of that Leave wandering the length of Greenhead Moss, away from people. His mind started playing tricks. I told him he was losing his grip. Of course, I didn't know what horrors men at the Front were experiencing then; no one at home did. He said he was probably going to be killed, and that I'd be a widow. We quarrelled violently. I said some unforgivable things. My Father insulted him and he left. I wanted to give him his ring back, but he refused to take it. That night he went on a drinking spree, met a girl and...."

"Ma Mother?"

She nodded.

"And ye never saw him again?"

"No, he came to me on his last Leave. Your Mother was pregnant and he was going to marry her. He...."

She paused, considering. Tommy could see there was more to tell.

"That's basically everything. Now you know!" she said with finality.

The fire had settled down to a dull glow. Outside the lamps were flickers of empty lives. There was no Moon.

Tommy stilled his questions. Somehow he knew that they would be inevitably answered.

She rose and switched on the lamp. The raw, strong tide of light swept away all the intimacy and secrets of the last few hours.

She hurriedly drew the blind. "Right, I'm sure you must be short of sleep, it's now past nine o'clock, so I think it's time you retired for the night. The Guest Bedroom is prepared."

"Miss, ah could fair go a guid doss, ah'm that tired ah could sleep on tap o a tanner," he responded frankly; and affirmed the truth of the statement by concluding it with a cavernous yawn.

She grinned faintly, "Quite!"

She led him into the bedroom on the other side of the Hall. A voluminous nightshirt lay spreadeagled over the counterpane.

"That's the best I can do for you I'm afraid. It belonged to my Father."

"Lovely, Miss." Tommy regarded the soft contours of the bed appreciatively. Half an hour later, he was snugly propped up in bed, drinking the last of his cocoa. He'd felt oddly coy when she had arrived with the steaming mug. Garbed in the nightshirt as he was, he'd pulled the counterpane up to his chin and blushed, a shy adolescent once more; afraid that she'd kiss him goodnight. She'd stared at him with a slightly guilty expression, then murmured, " Good night, I'll wake you at 7.30, I have to be out by 8.30 for school."

She'd tiptoed out as if he were already asleep.

Sleep was not long in coming. He switched off the light, put down his mug, and as the room winked into darkness around him, he was swallowed up into deep slumber.

CHAPTER 10

The wind skirled through the birks by the Kirk. Great wedges of dark cloud sailed across the sky, blotting out the stars.
A figure scaled the track up the Kirk Brae. The shadowy features were dim in the dark. A woollen cap topped the head, longish hair protruded. He wore a jacket, short breeches and long stockings.
Having reached the crest of the brae and peching with the effort, he stopped for a blow. His dark thoughts matched the landscape.
The Kirk Bae was aye a trauchle and he wasn't as young as he used to be. Ower auld to be stravaiging the hale laund riding ahint Claverhouse, 'Bluidy Clavers' as they caa'd him here in the heathen West. Little did they ken the man. A just, richt upstaundin chiel, better than the Covenanting dirt deserved.
A great, globed Full Moon fought its way clear of the cloud and illuminated the World with its silvery enchantment. The glinting path threaded the brae. The patter of his heart was returning to normal.
Twa months he'd spent in this bluidy toun, if ye could caa it that, bydin amidst the courss Covenanter folk. Still, noo the end o the tedisome task was at haund.
He'd been posted in Camnethan by Claverhouse himself to keep an eye on Kirk Attendance and to seek out information on local Covenanting unrest. Many in the vicinity had refused to take the Test. The area was a hotbed of potential rebellion. Tales had come of illegal religious gatherings hereabouts. Information had been hard to glean, but amidst the dour uncooperative folk, there were always a few willing to loosen their tongues somewhat if they could be plied with a sufficient quantity of guid ale. Persistent whispers of a fanatic preacher had started to filter through to him. This man seemingly had held Conventicles locally, and was preaching rebellion and sedition, as had happened at Drumclog a few years back. No one knew or would tell of the site of these gatherings. He knew that these were always held in out of the way desolate places, and instinct told him that locally Greenhead Moss was the likeliest location. He'd taken to wandering there, hoping to

encounter some evidence.

Most of the locals regarded him with deep distrust. In some eyes, the hatred of Fanaticism burned. But even the fanatics themselves realised that, as an agent of Claverhouse, dire retribution would fall on their shoulders if harm came their way.

Small companies of dragoons regularly made the rounds, and he sent a report through them to Captain Bell in Strathaven. Yes, he was safe enough, but to be sure it gave him little pleasure serving here in the damp West. He longed for the softness of his native Angus, away from the watchful eyes of the village folk.

Still after the morrow he'd have to thole it no more. He'd had a major success that day. He'd detected a change in atmosphere amongst the villagers in the past few days. A stirring, a vaguely concealed excitement. Backs were turned more theatrically than usual at his approach.

At his billet in the damp cottage of Mistress Wishart, an auld widow woman with no love for the Covenanters, he'd made his observations.

" Aye, he's comin richt enou," Mistress Wishart had replied tartly.

" Hoo div ye ken?" he'd asked.

" Thur's the stench o the Fanatic cratur aboot the place!" she snapped and would not say more.

He'd awakened and set off before dawn. He hid himself below the crest of a small knoll overlooking the main path into the Moss just beyond the Kirkyard. It was a canny decision. For once Fortune had favoured him. Just as a layer of grey pink tainted the lift, several shadowy figures, cloaked against the night, padded softly along the path. By the time the red-vapoured sun slunk above the eastern horizon, a goodly number of folk had passed.

After a short time, no one else appeared.

He waited a few moments, then set off in stealthy pursuit. The last stragglers were still in view, so keeping to the raised ground skirting the path, he lolloped along from tuft to tuft, keeping one eye open for bogs and the other on the uneven procession in front.

The worshippers; for now he had no doubt about what he had discovered, cut off the path at right angles and headed east, bathed in the ever strengthening rays of the sun.

He'd hunkered down again, ensuring that latecomers would not chance upon him. He was now confident of the general direction in which lay the illegal gathering, if such it was. He felt he could bide his time: it would be better to encounter the site when all present were engrossed in the Conventicle he had reasoned.

After a short while, he scanned the path from the village, and finding the coast clear, set off in the direction the worshippers had taken. It was easy to follow. The thirty or so folk he'd seen had trodden an easily detectable trail. He'd heard the Gathering before he saw it. A dark voice echoed over the treeless waste. He slunk behind a slight undulation, then wormed himself on his belly to the crest and stole a quick glance.

Below, a black garbed figure ranted and raved before the assembled company. All were engrossed in his diatribe: there seemed to be no sentinels scanning the Moss for intruders.

A further observation confirmed that the Preacher was unknown to him. A shilpit man with harshly angled features. Such a man would be easily recognisable if encountered again.

Quite a few members of the Congregation were well known to him. Gourlay, Inglis, Cadzow and Muir. Their presence was no surprise to him. But there in the front rank of the zealots was Johnnie Fairbairn, a chiel, one of the few, who often passed the time of day with him. Even Mistress Cowan the gravedigger's wife was there. How deep the poison of the Covenant ran in the veins of the Heathen West!

Still, he had smirked wryly in anticipation of the sight of the skellum Gourlay's face when he was arrested by Claverhouse's dragoons. The son of a hoor would wish he'd never been born!

Having amassed the information he required, he'd sneaked away without detection.

Only a faint doubt now dogged him. As he'd neared the main path, he'd caught site of Wull the Smith. He'd duked for cover, but had set up a whaup, its scraich enough to waken the dead. Realising that an attempt at concealment was in vain, he'd strode out onto the path and waved a cheery greeting to the Smith.

Wull, a dour sort of body, had grunted a gruff reply, but since that was his usual way, he'd not worried unduly about that. He'd then strode along the path whistling, perhaps overloudly, keeking round at intervals to ascertain Wull's location. Fortunately, Wull had proceeded along the main path, perhaps bound for the main peat diggings. As the village biggings hove into sight, he'd seen neither hide nor hair of anyone else.

He'd lain low for the rest of the day, not wishing to take premature action and so alert the miscreants to his discovery.

Whilst strolling through the village that afternoon, Fortune had again favoured him. He'd observed Gourlay and Inglis in rapt conversation with the well remembered figure of the Preacher himself. Inglis had noticed his approach and strode towards him, engaging him in a banal conversation, obviously meaning to distract him. Out of the corner of his een he spied Gourlay and the Preacher melt into Gourlay's house like snaw off a dyke.

He'd waited till dusk to slip down the Brae to Tam Shaw's in order to arrange a nag for the morrow, so that he could ride and personally report his discovery to Bell himself. The arrest of the Fanatic would be a feather in his cap. Indeed, it might be more than that: there had been a reward of 5000 merks paid out on the capture of the madman Cargill, him that had pronounced excommunication on the King, the Duke of York, and the Duke of Monmouth, and had stirred up sedition in this very locality. His heid had ended up on a spike on the Netherbow! Maybe this Fanatic had a price on his heid also.

Now however, with triumph in his grasp, he felt oddly uneasy.

It was a foul night. The chill wind rasped his lungs. Ower cauld for Merch. Once more the Moon was devoured by a great cowl of cloud. The wind plucked at his cap. He clutched the animated trunk of a birk, exhausted after his whirlwind day. He shut his eyes tight, trying to adjust to the totality of the dark.

Darkness blacker than the night.

A young man asleep on a luxurious bed: but restless and crying out, sweat beading his forehead.

He blinked open his eyes. What devilry was this?

Still the wind malagaroused, huffing amongst the birks. The great cloud was now silver rimmed at one end; announcing the reappearance of the Moon. Evil thoughts.

Was he right to betray the folk he had lived amongst these past few months, vile as they were? Perhaps they had the right of it; what with the Duke of York now Commissioner of Scotland and him a Papist.

He thrust away the thought. The very air hereabouts oozed the poison of their heresy.

He blinked out again into the darkness of his mind.

A dark horizon, last light lingering in the sky; the unmistakable profile of the western rim of the Valley. Suddenly the lift was aflame, a great red eye

75

pulsed, hurling away the dusk. A mighty straight winged bird was a mote in the eye. It flew a straight course, nary a flap of its wings, its voice a deep growl. T'was surely a chariot of God's Wrath. The western sky was stained with blood and slaughter. Surely a portent of Death and Destruction. He shook himself and broke into a cold sweat. The Vision had vanished. A malevolent trick of the mind. His unease grew to fever pitch.
Witchwood presences lurked amongst the birks. Someone was watching him. He whirled about, eyes crazed in the gurly dark.
The Moon burst through and five birks uprooted themselves, grew heads and encircled him. He crossed himself involuntarily.
" See how the creature returns to the fold o the Deil in the hour o his doom!" cackled one.
A great limb, glinting in the moonlight, struck out at him. He stepped back automatically, causing the sword to whizz down past his face, but his right foot exploded in fiery pain as it chopped through and buried itself in the earth.
He screamed, filling the night with his barbed agony. He staggered, and his life, now ending, flickered past as his assassins closed in for the kill.
Gourlay, eyes lit with blood lust, made ready to thrust. By his shoulder the Fanatic, satanic in the moonlight. He glanced behind and saw Muir, Cadzow and the Smith, his betrayer, all with swords in hand and ready to strike.
Realising the imminence of his doom, his lips formed a curse and he started forward to thrapple Gourlay in a death grip, but his mutilated foot refused to obey, and he swooned forward just as a heavy blow thudded into his thigh and a thrust from behind severed his spinal column and plunged into his brain. He died instantly, casting his unuttered death scream across the Centuries.
The room quailed as he screamed on and on.
A shaft of light. A panic stricken voice and the soft warmth of a body clinging to him.
" There, there, it's all right now."
Gentle hands caressed him, wiping his brow.
" It's all right now."
Warm lips kissed his cheek.
" It's all over," persuaded the soft female voice. " You're going to be all right. It was just a nightmare."

Eyes glazed with horror, Tommy sat up and looked about. Light flooded in from the Hall and illuminated the cosy spare bedroom. Abruptly he dissolved into an uncontrollable frenzy of weeping, grieving for the lonely, violent death of a lost soul.

" They murdered him," he sobbed at last, " ah saw it aw!"

" Who? Who was murdered?"

He stared straight at Miss Campbell, and declared firmly," The Man in the Moss!"

She gave a start. At that instant the bedroom door slammed, plunging the room into darkness. Instinctively she clung to him, holding her breath in terror.

After a moment she exhaled deeply. " I must have left a window open."

He resisted slightly as she disentangled herself, unwilling to surrender the warmth of her reality. She padded over to the door and allowed in the light once more. She smiled faintly from the Hall.

" I'm going to make some tea and kindle the fire." Her eyes hardened, "Then we'll go into the Lounge and you can tell me about your nightmare, if that'll help."

" It wis mair than a nightmare. It wis as if ah wis there hunners o years ago. It wis like bein inside his heid."

She paled, but said nothing, and made softly for the Kitchen.

In a short time the makings of a good blaze was sparking up the lum and he was clutching a steaming mug as he squatted before the fire. She was seated on the armchair, hypnotised by the fire.

" Are ye ready?"

She nodded imperceptibly.

He swiftly poured out the story of his vision, even including the names of the murderers.

At the end of the telling, she was still absorbed in the fire.

" Ye dinnae believe me," he said, crestfallen.

She did not look at him.

" No, that's not the case. I think I know now that what you've said is true," she said firmly.

" Are you sure you believe me?" he asked doubtfully.

She turned, eyes boring into him, " I know it's true!"

He waited; she had obviously more to say on the subject.

She swallowed hard, then began," I've told you that your father took to meandering the length and breadth of the Moss whilst on leave. He had a fascination about the place. Though we met at night after I had finished University, he spent most of the day there. He wanted to be apart from people, but there was more to it than just that.

Then one night he told me he'd seen an apparition. I asked him if it was a fallen comrade, but he said it was a man dressed in the period of the 17th Century."

Tommy jumped up, " The man ah saw murdered!"

" Yes, perhaps it was," she whispered.

" Whit happened then?" he demanded.

" I thought he was going mad. I told him to pull himself together. We quarrelled as I've said, and you know what happened then. Except on his last Leave he came to me. It turned out that he'd been hanging around the street waiting for me to appear. He was wild eyed and weeping. At first I tried to ignore him, but he would have caused a scene, and well, I still loved him, and life had been so empty without him."

Tears starred her eyes briefly, and she paused to soothe them away with her handkerchief before continuing.

" Then we walked for what seemed like half the day. As we strolled, a curious calm washed over him. It was as if a great weight had been lifted from his shoulders. He was not gay or devil-may-care; it was as if he was confident about himself once more. If he had been afraid or angry, he was no longer. With a strange smile of precognition, he told me he'd be killed back at the Front. I almost went into hysterics, but he just smiled. When I'd calmed, he told me that he knew, and that it would be all right. Of course, I couldn't believe my ears. But he said that he'd seen what would happen. 'It has been revealed to me and that is the way it must inevitably be.' Those were his very words.

" How could it be shown to you?" I'd remarked scornfully, and he replied that he'd seen a vision of the Future.

By that late period of the War, a little word of the effect of the shelling, gas and sheer Hell of the trenches had started to filter through to those of us at home. So by then I'd heard of some men who'd come home quite mad. Anyway, when I heard him say that, I humoured him, but he just smiled tiredly and said that in time I'd find out the truth of the matter.

But then our conversation was forgotten. Suddenly we were at the rim of the Valley, at the Horseley Brae just below Overtown. The Sun burst through at that instant, transforming the Valley into a fabulous, golden land. We entered its depths, and it was as if we'd conquered Time. Everything was the way it had been and everything would be all right. That was our stolen secret time. Sometimes it feels as if it lasts my whole life through. At times there's an enchantment on me; I can enter and we're together again there amidst the orchards."

Her eyes glazed over.

Then she smiled ironically, " Then we came out, and he told me he was getting married the next day. There was a girl and a bairn on the way.

It was eerie, but when he told me I wasn't surprised. It was as if some of his quiet peace had rubbed off on me, and he'd somehow implanted the knowledge into my brain.

Whilst I remained mute, he told me that he had to do the decent thing. He cared for the girl, but he loved me and would love me till the end of time. In a way, he said, we'd always be together.

Then he uttered a strange thing. He stated that the main reason he was going through with it was that his son to be born was important, and had a crucial task to perform."

" My Son has a crucial task to perform," she repeated, as she regarded Tommy through a haze of grief, wonder and enchantment.

" I never saw him alive again. He was killed a few months later at Cambrai shortly before the end of the War."

Her face was inscrutable.

" When I heard of your birth, I started to believe his tale, but of course it was too late then."

"So ye think the man in ma nightmare wis the one ma Da saw?"

There was a silence.

" I'm prepared to consider the possibility, I can't say more than that."

" Fair enough," he replied stoically.

He rose up, " Right, ah'd better get back tae bed, ah've kept ye up ower lang already."

She looked doubtful, " Are you sure? You might have more bad dreams."

" Aye, Miss," he said slowly," Ah dinnae think ah've anythin tae be feart of."

CHAPTER 11

Snug in the unaccustomed warmth of his new coat, Tommy cut through the morning bustle of the Main Street completely oblivious to it. It was a blue morning, but ice rimmed shower clouds plotted on the northern horizon.
At breakfast the conversation had not touched on the events of the previous evening. Tommy had revealed that there was a job on a farm open to him when he officially left the school, and that he was going to take it and join Rab. She had been downcast at this news, obviously she still had nurtured hopes that he might continue into Higher Education. When she mentioned this hope he'd simply said, " Ah have tae get away frae the hoose."
At this, a fierce light had entered her eyes.
" What shift is your Stepfather on today?" she had snapped at him.
" Two tae ten," he'd replied; but to his further question as to why she wished to know she had made no reply.
She'd told him to be back at her house by five o'clock to be in time for Tea, then as they were about to leave the house, she suddenly held him close in a fierce hug.
" Be careful up there. Do what you have to do, but keep your wits about you!"
As he blinked in surprise, she'd given him a quick peck on the cheek, then whisked him out the door. As he made his way along the Main Street, his cheek still beamed and her warm glow still clung to him.
And yet, she was up to something, but he couldn't work out what.
He stopped and took stock of his surroundings. He was in Stewarton Street, across from Chalmers Kirk and the Academy. Knots of small glum faces were dilly-dallying along the street. Playground hubbub throbbed on the wind. He inhaled a lungful of free air, momentarily appreciating the luxury of the situation; officially plunking the school.
So here he was, again heading for the Moss. There had been no conscious decision involved. It was funny how she'd known.
Now there was no rush. No voice hectored him; he was already ensnared. He thought about the murder he had witnessed: the oorie experience of

sharing someone's thoughts: the terror of being trapped in a murdered man's body. Only with the final coup de grace had he been set free from the enchantment.

But why had the voice of the murdered man echoed through Time? Why had the questing spirit sought him out? Perhaps his Father had experienced the same phenomenon. There had to be some connection with his Father. He had told Miss Campbell that he'd actually seen a phantom. As yet he himself had not. Perhaps their experiences were not the same.

He shook his head. His deliberations, as on previous occasions, were making no headway. Clearly, he concluded, it was his fate to be called thus, and in any case, he had a queerlike notion that some questions would be answered this day.

And yet as he strode through the normal town bustle, his steps gradually became leaden footed. The very normality of the scene gave wings to sudden doubt and perhaps fear. He didn't have to do this. He stalled, swithering. Surely the strain of recent events had affected his mind. Maybe he was turning into a daftie just like Wullie. He could easily go back and spend the day with Rab. Maybe some things were better left alone. But these visions had been so powerful. Which way?

After an age, or what seemed to be, he turned for home. As he did so, a voice, somewhat outlandish and indistinct, sounded behind him.

He'd vaguely been aware of a figure hovering at a close mouth nearby, but had paid no notice. An unkempt, thin-faced man, unshaven and dishevelled, regarded him. He was dressed in an old Army greatcoat, and looked down on his luck, like many others in these hard times. He seemed vaguely familiar. Tommy had the notion that he'd seen him around the town. He spoke again, but the words were garish and drony and hard to make out. Somewhat embarrassed, Tommy wrinkled his brows in bafflement. There was something wrong with the man's speech. Was he drunk?

The man spoke once more, more slowly, clearly trying to be precise. He pointed to Tommy, " You are Tom Neill's son." Tommy with concentration understood his words.

" Aye, how did ye know?"

The man shook his head. " Can't understand."

He pointed to his ears. " Deaf." he intoned.

Tommy regarded him somewhat warily. He'd never really experienced deaf folk before. But this man could speak; well after a fashion. He knew that most deaf people didn't speak at all; they waved their hands about and made strange grunts. Some people thought they were saft in the heid and made a fool of them.

The man produced a small writing pad and a pencil from his greatcoat, and started to write at great speed. He handed the pad to Tommy.

' Became deaf in the War. Shell.'

Tommy nodded and gestured for the pencil. ' How did you know me?' he wrote.

The conversation continued in like fashion, the man speaking the words he wrote. He scribbled rapidly, not writing in sentences.

' Was friend of your Father. In same regiment. HLI. Was on leave with Tom when he married your Mother. Knew her. Kept an eye on you.'

'What happened to you? Were you wounded?'

' Were attacking. Behind tanks. Wounded. Shrapnel. Bleeding to death in shell hole. Screaming.'

' Could you hear then?'

The man grinned wryly, " Yes," he spoke.

' Deaf now,' he wrote, ' no work. Do odd jobs. Home Fit for Heroes- Balls!!' He slashed the exclamation marks savagely. 'People think deaf folk are stupid and useless, but they're just the same as everyone else. Just can't hear. Lonely.'

He continued, now writing carefully in sentences, using an easy to read copperplate script. ' Before I enlisted I wanted to be a Teacher. I attended University with your Father, but I wasn't as clever as he. We enlisted together. The 16th H L I. The BB Battalion. We came through the Somme. Most of our pals were cut to pieces. Looked as though we'd see out the War together. Tom saved me. He ran out under heavy shelling, hauled me out and threw me over his shoulder. We'd almost made it to our Lines when a whizz bang copped us. Blew me into the trench. Came to in hospital. They'd stitched me up and somehow the wounds didn't get infected. But from then on can't hear. Thought I was out of my mind. Wanted to kill myself. Ear drums ruptured. Can't hear myself speak. Maybe I could hear a loud explosion, but that's all. Found out that Tom had been killed instantly.'

He paused, staring into space. 'Why did he come for me? He should have lived. Asked him why in the shell hole. Just said, " You're important," then told me to shut up.'

" Deaf now," he said, " can only talk with this."

He waved the pad and wrote,' Go to the Deaf Club in Glasgow when I have money for the train. They talk with their hands, in signs. Too fast. Only understand a little. Brain can't follow. Still they're kind to me. Can finger spell though. That's easy.'
' Finger spell?'
He held up his hand and pointed to each finger- A, E, I, O, U; then made shapes of the consonants B, C, D and so on through the alphabet.
' Slow though. Maybe born deaf people think I'm stupid too. I don't fit anywhere.'
He shook his head ruefully, ' Well need to go. Labouring jobs maybe going down at the Stenton. If not the Missioner at the Club said he'd try to get me a job in Bookbinding or Furniture making. They run a workshop, but there's a waiting list. Born deaf at the top of the list. Maybe have to travel. Nothing for deaf people here.'
He looked Tommy straight in the eye. 'I wanted to shake your hand. Your Father gave his life for me, so I must try to make the best of it. I'm Important!'
He shook his head in bafflement, then held Tommy's hand in a firm grasp.
" Where are you going now, son? Not at school?" he said, his words now clearer to Tommy.
Tommy shrugged in confusion, " I'm not sure."
" Maybe you're important too," said the man. He waved and set off as Tommy pondered deeply.
After a moment he dashed after the veteran, tapped him on the shoulder, and gestured for the pad.
' What's your name?'
" Sam," said the old soldier with a faint smile.
Tommy watched Sam as he wandered off on his lonely quest for a living wage. He turned again towards the Moss, finally sure that this was where his path lay.
He made a leisurely ascent up to the margins of the Moss. By the Perchie, he stopped for a blow. He lifted his eyes to the far horizons of his world.
Tintock with its muckle skull cairn, the sleeping Lord of the Valley. The day, he thought, would come again, when that dark mountain would stretch out its frozen paws into the Valley once more, scouring and grinding its flanks to dust.
Icy cloud citadels slunk above the Campsies, stalking with the wolf wind

towards Glasgow: harsh Winter ambushes for the city dwellers.
As he savoured the great sweep of the land, he fancied that he detected the majestic, imperiously slow beat of the World's heart, and that he was an infinitesmal but integral part of it. For this instant in Time and Space, he was at one with the Earth, and felt its stately ballet as it turned about itself and danced its pirouette through the realms of infinite dark. This was the Deep Reality: all else: all our deeds and doings, were consumed as transient sparks in the never ending fire.
Far off, the bogle wail of a work's siren: a lost soul in torment.
The Wind stabbed him in the back. Slowly he smiled and turned to face the elemental adversary. The chill lift was a clear blue empty canvas. A day's work to be carried out.
Water hens huddled at the margins of the Perchie. He thought of the drowned dog he'd discovered just a few days before. Perhaps it had been a portent. Now his way seemed clear.
He headed for the great stone. In its vicinity, he knew, lay the hub of his enchantment.
As he drew near, the Wind's blatter eased. It was as if he'd wandered into a great eye of calm; a doldrum of Time and Space. Expectantly, he waited. Nothing, hardly a breath of wind.
He concentrated, closing his een tight shut against the World, trying to call up a whisper from the grim regions of the Past. But only a grey chiaroscuro of blurry impressions coiled in his mind's eye. He held, transfixed, grappling with formless shapes in the mists, but could not penetrate Time's gyres.
A douce breath of air soughed in his ear, summoning him back to the light of day. The impression of calm, if it had ever in truth existed, had evaporated. He daunnered a vague circuit round the Stane. The chuff of a distant locomotive enhanced the impression of normality.
He was bamboozled. What was he doing up here traipsing around like a fusionless gowk? Incongruously, he blushed, and whummled round to see if anyone was observing his daftness. Why had he paid such attention to his nightmares? He'd been upset by the events at home and at school, he told himself. This had made the dreams so fearsomely realistic. Now he knew there had been no reality in them. His mind had been playing tricks. Perhaps his Father had been seeing things too. There was nothing here and nothing would happen, so he'd been wasting his time. He was free of the weird nightmares. He'd broken their hold on him.

Vauntily, he louped on the broad back of the Stane, half aware that up till now he'd been giving it a wide berth. Gallusly, he straddled it. He was master of his own destiny again.

Only a few days previously he'd sat on the knoll at the other side of the Moss, reflecting on the Future. Then it had seemed mirk and threatening. But now the last tendrils of doubt had evaporated under the empty arms of the sky.

He was at the end of an era. In less than two weeks he would take up the mantle of manhood. Now he was ready to cross the boundary. He opened his mouth wide and hurled a wild scraich of freedom into the lift.

Off guard, he was clawed back into the bowels of Time. The day winked out and a veil of dark night swirled over him. A cloud tossed Moon glimmered through a frame of waving branches. There was danger close at hand. He tensed, moulding himself into the trunk of a birk. He looked down at himself. He was indeed himself; there in his own clothes, shivering in the dreichness of a far gone night.

The startled crack as of an axe nearby. The birks cringed. Again. Thunk! Thunk! A dark figure crashed through the undergrowth. The shadow loomed and passed.

" Whit fur kin we no lee him alane whaur he ligs?" grumbled a voice.

" D'ye want tae bring the Deil doon on oor shoothers!" was the courss rejoinder," yase yur noddle man; the word'll be oot that he wis murdert!"

Tommy's feet made no sound as he slunk through the undergrowth towards the voices. Beyond the Kirk, bathed in moonlight, were five figures. At their feet lay another, crumpled like a sack.

" Ah've hewed sax muckle snags o birk."

A clatter of branches were flung down unceremoniously by the corpse.

The tallest figure bent down to examine them. With a grunt he whurled one into the branches close to Tommy. He ducked instinctively.

" That yin's nae guid!" The man straightened up; a long faced man, hair hanging limp to his shoothers.

A smaller man with ragged top hose knelt over the body. A knife glinted in his hand. He seemed to hack at the feet of the corpse. With a satisfied grunt, he straighted up and secreted something under the folds of his cloak.

" Nae sense in feedin twa braw buckles tae the worms."

The larger man spat in disgust. " Bi Goad, ye're a whitterick, Cadzow; takin the buckles frae a deid man's shin!"

Cadzow shrugged.

" Whaur are we takin him?" interjected a third voice.

The others immediately turned to regard the last of the group, who stood swathed in a black cloak, staring into the blackness beyond the Kirk. The sombre figure merged into the dark, part of the very night itself. Tommy was surprised. He had gained a definite impression that the lank cadaverously featured man was the leader of the group.

The man turned to face the others. His face seemed to bleize in the moonlight. Tommy recognised the harsh visage immediately. It was the fanatic Preacher of his dream. Awed by the presence of the man, Tommy quailed behind the trunk of a birk, not daring to look.

" Ah ken a fitting lair fur an agent o the Deil!" snickerered the voice of the Preacher. " Richt, heize him up!"

Even fear could not restrain Tommy's curiosity any longer. He keeked out prudently.

The flichtering star of a lantern was now brandished by the Preacher. Two of the others hoisted up the corpse. He saw that it was the body of a grey bearded man with whiskers pointed at the chin. Curly hair tumbled down below a woollen cap as the head dangled. Tommy grued as a slorach of gore and brains drooled from a gaping wound in the back of the neck. For an instant, as they pivoted the head towards him, the still wide open eyes seemed to spark alive and stare entreatingly towards him.

" Gie me up thur snags!" commanded the tall man.

He was handed the branches, which he cradled under his oxter.

" Richt," announced the Preacher," ah'll guide."

Holding aloft the lantern like some dark Messiah, he strode into the night, leaving the others to shamble after him.

Tommy hesitated, reluctant to quit the cover of the birks. For the first time he became aware of the eldritch nature of the apparent reality of the vision. He gripped the trunk of a birk. It felt real and solid. He inhaled the night air. Chill and dreich. A sharp blast of wind ripped through the close aisles of the trees. His foot pawed at the ground. dead leaves crunkled.

He had been precipitated from one gyre of Time to another. What was the nature of his existence here? Could he come to harm?

The Moon was consumed once more. A Will o the Wisp danced ayont the Kirk, growing fainter. The oorie light beckoned. He had been sent as a Seer: the vision was not ended.

He stepped out from the shaw into the naked dark and slunk after the murderers: the Preacher, Gourlay, Muir, Cadzow and the Smith, he now remembered.

He imagined himself a shadowy wraith, but the squelch of his feet on the waterlogged ground seemed to give the lie to the notion.

Still the lantern lured him through the glaur and mire. He kept what he judged to be a canny distance from the shadowy funeral procession on the edge of the werelight.

At one point, one of the bearers stumbled just ahead. The body sprawled to the ground with a mucky splash. The other bearer instinctively let go of the feet. Tommy cooried down, holding his breath.

With a curse, Muir, who had been taking the heavy head end of the body, picked himself up. The others used this as an excuse to stop for a breather. With an air of testiness the Fanatic joined them.

Gourlay glowered into the dark in the general direction of Tommy.

" Ah've a queerlike notion that whyles thur's someboby ahint us!"

Tommy huddled down further, pressing hid face into the muck.

" Bogles i the daurk?" sneered Cadzow, getting some of his own back, " thur's naethin there!"

" Haud yur whisht!" rapped the Fanatic," mak haste, it's nae faur noo!"

The macabre procession penetrated into the Stygian depths of the Moss. Tommy tracked cautiously, a miasma of mist licking at his heels.

Abruptly, the flitting will o the wisp stilled. Tommy hunkered low, then worked himself forward on to a slight undulation just outside the margin of the circle of light.

Dramatically, the Preacher was gesticulating at a muckle rock which lay adjacent like a slain beast.

Muir interrupted his flow, "Thur's ill luck aboot this place. Whit wey div we hae tae come here aside the Wutch Stane?"

" We sall gie back the Deil his ain!" intoned the Fanatic grandly.

" But fowk tell that bogles and wutches gether here tae commune wi the Deil. They could howk up the boady an cause it tae walk!" stammered the Smith, craning over his shoother nervously.

The Fanatic regarded him with irritation. " Aye, ah've nae doot that heathen blasphemies wur carriet oot here in faur off days, but an agent o Satan kin no hae a Christian burial. He's pairt o the 'Kingdom o Darkness' that must be overthrown, as the Declarations say. Let him lie here, an may his Sowl

roast in Hell!"
He raised his arm and indicated a spot several yards distant from the Wutch Stane. He produced a spade from under the voluminous folds of his cloak.
" Howk ower yonder!" he commanded, handing the spade to the Smith.
Reluctantly, he thrust the spade into the peaty earth. He worked swiftly, with nervous anxiety. In a short time a shallow grave was excavated.
The savage gash in the back of the head wept as the body was lowered gingerly into the grave.
Grim faced, the Smith lunged the spade into Cadzow's hands.
" Yird him!" he growled.
Cadzow made to reply, then thought better of it and spattered a spadeful of earth over the corpse.
" Hing oan," interjected Gourlay, raising his hand. Gathering the five cut branches of birk, he placed them carefully over the body.
" Whit fur ur ye daein that?" asked Muir.
" The birk'll stoap the ghaist frae walkin," Gourlay replied, backing off from the grave. Instinctively, his hands made a sign to ward off evil spirits.
" Ailbins ah wis wrang when ah seyed it wis juist in the faur off days that Satanic Blasphemies wur carriet oot hereaboots," the Preacher muttered tellingly.
Gourlay flushed, but made no reply. He turned his back as if to blot out the memory of his crime.
Cadzow deftly began to scatter the spill over the corpse. The others, save Gourlay, watched as if hypnotised.
Gourlay, meanwhile, cast his eyes to the gurly lift. At that instant, the western horizon pulsated with sudden light. The sky ran with blood. A dark Nemesis bird cut through the light.
The terror of Hell burnished in his eyes, Gourlay made to cry out. As he did so, his fear stricken eyes rested on the startled features of Tommy.
Gourlay's mouth formed a scream just as the mighty wind of Time plucked Tommy from the scene. A whorling kaleidoscope of dark and shadow fled as light glinted, then seared over him.
Peewit! Peewit!
A peesie jinked about the sky.
The Wutchstane slumbered beneath him, its hidden power dormant.
The landscape seemed unchanged. No one was in the vicinity. The Sun appeared to have altered its position not a whit. Nothing to indicate the

passage of time.

He looked down at himself. His clothes were smudged with great dollops of glaur, and his knees were damp from kneeling down. His head swam. There was no doubting the reality of what he had witnessed.

He swung his legs gingerly off the Wutchstane. As he eased himself away, his hand tingled violently as a jolt of elemental power seemed to surge from the stone. He backed off hurriedly

" Bi Goad, ah'm gettin masel oot o here," he breathed. He turned on his heels to skelp off.

The figure of a man stood nearby, his back to Tommy. He blinked in surprise; he could have sworn he'd been alone. Slowly his features set in a smile.

" Wullie, whit are ye daein here?"

The figure made no response. Sudden doubt pounded at his heart. He looked closer.

A man with a green woollen cap, long hair protruding at the base. A grey jacket, top hose and short leather breeches.

He quivered in realisation.

A black cape of blood radiated from a savage rent in the bonnet.

An irresistible force propelled him towards the spectre. An echo in the ebb and flow of Time, the apparition stared lifelessly in to the west. As he drew close the Vision began to lose its solidity. The air churned, and it seemed to wither into the ground.

Freed from its hold, he fled randomly, howling with the trauma of what he had witnessed.

Air and Earth seemed to coalesce as the World's treadmill spun round beneath his frantic flight.

A rough hand plucked him up as a dark mass was about to envelop him. Briefly, he was suspended in mid air. Softly, a cloud traversed his line of vision. A soft voice twittered in his ear.

" Son, are ye ettlin tae dae away wi yersel?"

Wullie looked down at him anxiously. Slowly, his eyes focussed on reality. He blinked and relaxed momentarily.

" Are ye aw richt?" enquired Wullie.

The blind panic flowed once more across Tommy's features. He jumped up, grabbing hold of Wullie's coat.

" Wullie, Wullie, ah've juist seen..." He hesitated for an instant, then went off at a tangent.

" Ah ken aw aboot how it happened; he wis murdered, an ah've juist..."
Wullie nodded.
" Aye," he murmured.

CHAPTER 12

There was a sharp rap at the door; a rap smacking of Officialdom, thought Agnes. She tarried, mentally questing for sources of trouble.
" Haw Ag!" bellowed Geordie, still ensconced in the bed in the back room, " ye no gaun tae answer yon bluidy door?"
" Aye, ah'm juist gaun, Son," she answered in a placatory tone.
She shrugged and eased open the door.
A smartly dressed lady regarded her intently.
" Eh aye, whit is it?" asked Agnes, somewhat taken aback.
" Mrs Brawley?" The lady spoke in an educated tone.
" Aye," replied Agnes, somewhat defensively.
" I've come to see you and your husband regarding your son Tommy."
" Whit aboot him?" Agnes demanded, now openly suspicious.
"I'm Miss Campbell, one of his teachers at school."
" His teacher?" Agnes was incredulous.
" His English teacher," added Miss Campbell.
" Aw aye, ah've heard him speak o ye. Ye're the yin that gies him books tae read."
" Yes." She smiled faintly.
" An whit is it that ye want? He's no here ye ken. Ah dinnae ken whaur he is, an that's a fact." A hint of worry intruded.
" Yes I'm aware of that, that's why I want to speak to you."
" How d'ye....." She cut off in mid sentence.
Something about the woman was extremely familiar, calling up the deep forgotten past.
" Ah ken ye, ye're the lassie that....."
" Yes, Tommy's father was engaged to me before he met you," stated Miss Campbell with cool frankness.
Agnes slammed the door in her face.
An instant later a determined knock reverberated through the house.
" Whit's aw this?" came an angry voice from the back room.
" Mind yer ain business!" snapped Agnes.

Another rap at the door.
Ready to launch a tirade of abuse, Agnes hurled the door open.
" Well, are you going to keep me on the step or shall we have our discussion in private?"
Miss Campbell coolly inclined her head towards the next landing where Lizzie McKay and Bessie Chalmers looked on with obvious interest.
Agnes flushed and bit her tongue.
" Come in," she said roughly. As she ushered Miss Campbell inside, she paused to look daggers at Lizzie and Bessie before she slammed the door.
" Sit doon." She gestured at the chair by the fire.
" Thank you. I'll come straight to the point; it's my Lunch Hour, and I haven't much time." She paused briefly as she sat down.
" I know that Tommy's sleeping rough, and I don't want the situation to continue."
" Oh dae ye no?" Agnes drew herself up to her full height. " An whit business is it o yours anyway?"
" The welfare of my pupils is my concern," replied Miss Campbell icily.
" Richt, whit's gaun oan here?" Geordie stood in the doorway, dressed only in his breiks and semmit.
Miss Campbell scanned his unkempt features with ill concealed distaste. One side of his face was still livid in the aftermath of the burning incident.
" Mr Brawley I presume?"
" Aye, who wants tae ken?"
" Miss Campbell, Tommy's teacher," she replied tartly.
Immediately his attitude became somewhat deferential.
" Oh aye, whit kin ah dae for ye, Mistress?"
She did not mince her words, " I want you to allow Tommy back into the house."
He sorted, " Aye that will be right! The meenit ah clap ma een on yon wee shite ah'm gaun tae gie him the bleachin o his life. D'ye see whit he did tae me?"
He thrust his savagely burned face at her.
" Yes I know all about that, and believe you me he's desperately sorry about the whole affair."
" Ah'll desperate him. Ah had even tae get treatment frae the Doctor. Cost me fower shullins so it did."
She opened her handbag and rummaged in her purse. She withdrew two

half crowns and handed them to him.
" Take this; it will cover your medical expenses."
He blinked in surprise, then swiftly pocketed the coins.
" Now," she continued," I want him to be able to come back here in perfect safety. It will only be for less than two weeks anyway."
" Whit d'ye mean twa weeks?" demanded Agnes.
" Well he's starting his job then, isn't he?"
" Whit joab?"
" You mean you don't know about it?"
" Ah dinnae ken aboot ony joab."
" Why his job on the farm. He starts a week on Monday." Miss Campbell was puzzled. " Didn't he tell you? Oh, perhaps he hasn't seen you since he decided to take it."
Agnes's brows darkened. " A fine thing, tae hear aboot yer son's joab second haund!"
" Obviously he meant to tell you as soon as he saw you." She regarded Geordie accusingly, "If he'd been allowed in the house, I'm sure you'd have been the first to know."
Agnes's eyes flashed, " Ye think ah dinnae care aboot ma boy! Ye come in her wi yer swanky claes an big words. Whit dae ye ken aboot bringin up a boy? Ah'll warrant ye've nae weans o yer ain!"
Miss Campbell withered momentarily, then said quietly, " That may be, but in my job I've had more children through my hands than you'll ever see. Anyway, this isn't the point. I'm well aware of your situation. I'm not here to criticise you in any way. I know times are hard, and it's difficult to make ends meet."
Agnes sneered, "Aw aye? Ah don't see _you_ sufferin!"
Miss Campbell's facade of calm finally snapped, " There are many ways to suffer. You had the person I most wanted in my whole life, so don't complain to me!"
Agnes smirked triumphantly, " Aye, ah did didn't ah." Her face fell," But Ah didnae have him for ower lang."
A softness grew in the Teacher's face, " No, perhaps we're suffering together." They regarded each other, a transitory kinship forming a bond between them.
" But you have Tommy," murmured Miss Campbell.
" Aye." Agnes nodded and turned to Geordie. " C'mon Son, let him come

back intae the hoose."

" He'll apologise for what he did. Anyway it's only for a short time," coaxed Miss Campbell," then he'll be off to the farm. He promises to send you a good share of his wages," she added astutely.

" Aye, ah should bluidy well think so!" He had been neatly sidetracked. When it came to the crunch his greed overcame his desire for revenge.

" Aye he can come, as lang as he keeps oot o ma wey, but if he steps oot o line ah'll...."

" You'll do nothing of the sort. If you harm him, I'll have the Authorities down on your back quicker than you can blink!" shouted Miss Campbell.

" Are you threatenin me?" he growled

" No," she replied in a more conciliatory tone, " it won't come to that. You have my personal guarantee that he'll behave himself."

He humphed at that, and mustering what was left of his dignity, he retreated to the back room to get ready for his shift.

Agnes smirked at his departure. " Big wean," she muttered. " Men! There only guid for wan thing, an no even that!"

" I hear you have a bit of a hard time with him," nodded Miss Campbell sympathetically.

" Och, ah can haunle him!" snorted Agnes.

" Yes, I've no doubt you can. Well, I'm glad all this is settled."

" Aye." A queer far away look entered her eyes.

"Ye ken Miss Campbell....."

" My friends call me Jinty," smiled Miss Campbell.

" Ye ken, eh Jinty, ah've often wished that Tom had never taen up wi me yon nicht, an marriet ye as he wis gaun tae. It wis aye you he cared for."

" Yes....I know that. But it was as if something was driving him to act the way he did; something beyond our understanding."

She shook her head. " Well, what's done is done." She noticed the time. " Well I must be off."

Swiftly and unexpectedly, Agnes gave her a quick hug. " Thanks for comin Jinty," she whispered.

Surprised pleasure flitted across Miss Campbell's face. " I'm glad to be of help, em....Agnes. I'll see he's home this evening. Your husband will be out at work then, so that will make things easier for you."

Her eyes quested round the room and rested on a large encyclopaedia protruding from beneath Tommy's bed. Her eyes misted over.

She fled from the room, pausing only on the threshold to sob," Look after yourself now."
Agnes looked vexed, and spoke as if Miss Campbell were a child, " Hurry up Hen, or ye'll be late." She stood on the step and looked after her anxiously as she strode back to the everyday world from the barbed corridors of Time.
Lizzie and Bessie still gossiped two stairs up, pretending not to notice the tableau below.
Agnes stared for an age, lost in the restless heavens, then, unaware of their presence, she turned into the house and closed the door softly.

CHAPTER 13

" Ah dinnae want tae go back!" Tommy shook his head vehemently.
It was five o'clock that evening. They stood by the fire in Miss Campbell's lounge.
" It'll be all right. I've seen to everything. You'll be in no danger from your Stepfather."
" Ah never want tae clap eyes on him again. Ah'd much rather stey here wi you!" he blurted out.
" That wouldn't be right. You've only another wee while to go at school and then you start your job. You should spend the time with your family. Your Mother's anxious to see you."
An anguished look spread over his features. Abruptly, he clung to her and crushed himself into her breasts. " Can ah no stey wi ye?" he sobbed.
She looked down at the crumpled, tear stained face of the son of her lost love. She felt his body hard against her. A sudden impulse made her lift his chin up. She made to kiss him, then stopped and shook her head. God, how she wanted him to stay.
" No," was what she said. " Your Mother needs you." Gently, she disentangled him.
" All right," he said resignedly.
" That's the spirit. Anyway, tomorrow's the Equinox; the first day of Spring. Spring will be a grand time to be on the farm."
" Equinox?"
" Yes. The day on which the Sun is directly overhead at the Equator. The day when day and night are both equal."
" So Winter's ower for another year?"
" Yes," she smiled," the Winter's over."
He made for the door. " Ah'll need tae get ma things."
He paused at the threshold. " Can I come to visit you?" he asked formally.
" Of course, anytime: and you can start later this evening when you collect the remainder of your clothes. They're not all ironed yet. I'll have them ready for you later. Anyhow I want to hear how you got on."

He beamed as she showed him out the front door.
" Oh Tommy!" she called him back.
" Aye Miss?"
" Did you go to the Moss Today? Did you....?"
" Aye Miss." A shadow crossed his face. His tongue grew guarded. " But there's still work there tae be done yet."
Her brows wrinkled momentarily. She could see that he didn't wish to elaborate.
" All right. Be careful though. Anyway get on your way. I believe your Mother might have some Tea ready for you."
" Right, Cheerio! See you later Miss!" he called as he sped along the Terrace. In two minutes flat he was skelping along Smith's Land. He paused outside the window. His Mother was peeling tatties by the bunker. Something made her look up. Their eyes met and her face lit up. Tommy breinged for the door.

CHAPTER 14

> 'Wae's me, wae's me.
> The acorn's no yit
> Faaien frae the tree,
> That's tae grow the wid,
> That's tae mak a cradle,
> That's tae rock the bairn,
> That's tae grow a man,
> That's tae lay me.'
> *(Scots Anonymous)*

The Sun was arcing its great sweep to the western horizon as two figures strode towards the Wutch Stane. One perched a spade on his right shoulder, but the other was not similarly encumbered.

After his encounter with the spectre the previous day, Tommy had accompanied Wullie to his hut. Wullie had boiled a billie over the fire for him and fed him a doorstep of bread slabbered with jam.

Tommy had made to tell him about what he had witnessed, but Wullie had shaken his head.

" Whisht noo. There's deeds to be done yet. There'll be time for the tellin then."

He cast his eyes at the disc of the Sun and intoned in a stentorian voice, "The Circle is not yet complete!"

Tommy started. Such speak was completely out of character for Wullie.

" Whit d'ye mean?" he demanded.

Wullie gave him an enigmatic glance, " Ye'll find oot."

As the fire flickered, Tommy sat alternatively swathed in warmth then cold as the wind blustered away the fire's radiance,

At last he understood. His role was clear. It had fallen to him to release the soul from its torment. He knew where the body lay. Now he could free it from its hidden grave and reveal the murder that had been committed to the light of the World.

In the distance he had spied the unmistakable figure of Gerry Rolink traipsing back to the peat hag after his dinner.

An idea whispered at him. Surely it would be better if he was accompanied whilst he searched for the body. Gerry was always looking for new diggings. Perhaps he could direct him to the area for a trial dig.

He glanced round at Wullie as he formed airy megaliths of near-dried peat. Surely though, he should ask Wullie first of all.

" Wullie, ah need tae dae a bittie howkin aside the Wutch Stane. Will ye gie me a wee haund?" he asked hesitantly, unconsciously utilising the ancient term for the Stone.

" Wutch Stane is it? Ah'm no gaun near it. Ah cannae help ye Son!" He shook his head repeatedly. " Ah cannae help ye. It's no up tae me!"

Now the Wutchstane lay in wait atop the rise. Tommy, leading the way, halted at a drainage channel. He turned to his companion.

" This is juist a wee yin. Ye can loup it nae bother."

Gerry Rolink, a wee wiry man, still retained a youthful countenance. He took off his bunnet and wiped his deeply tanned brow. Gerry's parents were Hollanders, who had migrated to Scotland for the work many years before. His speech was as broad as the next man, only occasionally did a slight thickness of accent betray his ancestry.

" Oh is that right? Ah'm no as souple as ah used tae be, ye ken."

" Och it's puff candy. Watch me dae it."

Tommy paced backwards, then took a dramatic running jump. But in his overconfidence, he mistimed his jump, and his rear foot thudded into the bank below the edge. Frantically, he scrambled with his knee and his other leg, succeeding in crumbling away a large chunk of the edge before he managed to stand upright. He looked over at Gerry shamefacedly. Gerry shook his head.

He flung over his spade, took four paces backwards, then bounded athletically over the channel, clearing it by a good three or four feet. He retrieved his spade and smirked at Tommy.

" Aye, maybe ah can teach ye young yins something yet!" he chuckled quietly. " Right," he continued, " where is the place ye were speakin aboot?" In fact, it had been relatively easy to persuade Gerry to investigate this new site, though he had insisted that it had to wait until the end of the day's shift. His current bank was all but exhausted.

Tommy had spun a tale of rich, dark peat outcropping near the surface by an ancient peat hag. Though there was an old peat bank, the former part of his statement was speculative to say the least. Still, it was possible that good peat lay below the surface.

Now Tommy pointed straight at the Wutchstane.

" It's just ower there ablow the Stane!"

Gerry looked vaguely uncomfortable. He scanned around .

" Are ye comin then?" Tommy demanded, impatiently striding onward.

Gerry made no move to follow.

" Ah've been ower this wey a few time, but ah dinnae care for the feel o the place."

Tommy's mind raced, but his features remained non-committal.

" Whit d'ye mean?" he said casually.

Gerry looked flustered. " Weel it's like doon by the Auld Pit, where the explosion killt aw thae folk in the aulden times."

Tommy maintained his facade of innocence. " But there never wis a Pit ower here."

Gerry blushed, " Naw, but it's juist...." His voice trailed off in confusion.

" Are ye comin well?" persisted Tommy.

Gerry sighed, " Aw richt, lead on."

As they neared the site, Tommy recalled with a shudder the gaunt figure of the spectre as it had sprouted into the light of the Present from the dark earth of the Past. He superimposed his mind's eye view of the apparition on to the terrain until he obtained what he thought was the correct correlation. He screwed his eyes in concentration, and momentarily the air seemed to shimmer above a slash of verdant turf a few yards distant. That was the spot!

Gerry, meantime, was eyeing the crumbled outline of the old peat bank appraisingly. He made ready to start a trial excavation.

" Ower here Gerry!" urged Tommy.

Gerry looked round, somewhat irritated.

" Naw, Son, this looks like a guid spot. Guid peat here."

" Naw! naw!" implored Tommy," Here'll be better!" He gesticulated violently at the patch of ground at his feet. " Try here! Try here!"

Gerry wrinkled his brow, surprised at the lad's vehemence.

" The best peat'll be here, rich and daurk ah'm tellin ye!"

Gerry reluctantly hoisted his spade over his shoulder and trudged towards the spot, drawing Tommy an odd look.

"Here!" indicated Tommy.

"Aye, dinnae yatter on, ah heard ye the first time." He regarded the spot testily, then glanced at the Sun. Time was getting on.

Might as well humour the boy, then all the quicker to get loused for the day he thought. He spat on his hands, rubbed them together, then sliced through the earth. He levered out a spadeful, laid it down and examined it. Beneath the thin surface layer was peat; a fine layer of light brown, a thinner layer of decayed peat vegetation, then below was the beginnings of a layer of dark brown fibrous stuff.

Perhaps the boy was right. It would need double digging though. He glanced at Tommy, but he was no longer beside him. Looking up the rise, he blinked as he located him, cowering behind the Stane as if suffused by fear. What ailed the boy? He began to wonder whether some of Hairy Wullie's daftness had rubbed off on him. He shook his head and set to the howking with a will.

Tommy had bolted, unable to stand the suspense. He hid behind the bulk of the Wutchstane. It seemed to blot out the World. He buried himself into its depths. What if Gerry found nothing? Then all the phenomena of the past week were but mischievous tricks of his mind and he was surely daft.

The sound of a spade biting into the earth.

If though, the body was indeed there, what then?

The Stane seemed to cloak itself about him.

'Then the Circle is complete,' it answered.

A stirring in the eternal Dark. A churning in my earth prison. The dark dissolves around me. Now! Claw my way upwards into Light!

The snap as of a branch breaking.
A grunt of annoyance.
"Whit's this?"
Tommy sprang up and tumbled down the rise.
"Whit've ye found?"
Gerry looked out from his trial pit. He'd cut a section six feet square, and had begun to dig to the lower level. He pulled out a protruding length of branch. He scanned it briefly.
"Birk," he announced and tossed it aside. He peered into the hole.
"There's somethin under it."

Tommy stepped down beside him.

" Whit is it?"

Below the snapped off length of birk was a mass of greenish cloth. Gerry bent down and tugged at the material.

" A bit o auld rag or somethin. Whit's it daein unner the peat?"

He turned to Tommy mystified.

Tommy looked solemn.

Gerry tugged at the material once more.

" There's mair, it goes richt unner. Ah'l have tae dig it oot."

He eased away another spadeful of peat. Gingerly, he extracted the rest of the birk branch. A disc was fastened to the cloth below.

" A button! a metal button. This must be a jaikit!"

" Aye," mumbled Tommy," it wis."

Gerry darted a look at him.

" How d'ye ken?" he snapped warily.

Tommy made no reply, but stared down, deep into the past.

With feverish care, Gerry eased away the peat. A framework of branches was revealed, and below, a green belted garment with a row of buttons was clearly discernible.

" It's a hale jaikit!" gasped Gerry

A darker material loomed out from the base of the Jacket. Gerry took away two more spadefuls and bent to examine it.

" It's leather; maybe these are breiks."

Something protruded from the material. Uneasily, Gerry touched the object. With a cry of fright, he sprang out of the pit, the colour drained from his face.

Coolly, Tommy hunkered down and clawed away the peat.

A bone. Darkly stained by the peat, but unmistakably a bone. A thigh bone. He looked over at Gerry.

" A bone," he announced.

Gerry crossed himself. "Holy Mither o Goad, it's a human body. Somebody's buried doon there!"

Tommy took up the spade which Gerry had tossed aside in his panic. He delved away the peat from the area of the shoulders and head. He caught his breath. There was the well-remembered woollen cap. Fingers tingling, he cleared away more peat.

Only the top of the skull remained below the cap; some of it crumbled in his fingers. He could see a straggle of long greying hair emerging from below the cap.

A sudden gust plucked at him, whirling the dust into the air. With a startled cry a snipe shot up from a damp tussock only yards away. It zig-zagged in a spiralling loop about the lift, rejoicing in its mastery of the air. Higher and higher it rode the wind, then fell to earth imperceptibly, far to the west. Startled to his feet by the sudden flight of the bird, Tommy watched it descend and slowly recovered his composure.

He breathed deeply and announced, " Ah've found the skull."

Gerry backed away even further.

" Whit wey would anybody be yirdit oot here in the middle o the Moss?" Unspoken thoughts shone in his eyes.

" He wis murdered, that's how," Tommy said softly.

" Murdered!" Gerry's face grew grey. " We'll need tae get the Polis!"

He sidled away.

Tommy stepped out of the pit. " Ah'll stey here an uncover the hale o the body."

Gerry regarded him as if he were bewitched and gasped incredulously, " Ye'll stey?"

" Aye, we'll maybe no find the place again if we baith go," replied Tommy, knowing full well that there was no danger of that whatsoever.

" Oh aye, maybe ye're richt."

He took to his heels in the general direction of Waterloo.

" Gerry, where are ye gaun? Go up tae Newmains; the Polis Station there's the nearest." Wild eyed, Gerry took his bearings, then veered madly to the East towards Newmains.

The Moss was silent as Tommy set to work revealing the body. In a short time he was done.

Mainly the clothes remained. Cap, jacket, breiks, shoes and stockings were well preserved. The cap and a shoe were savagely gashed where the swords had cut into them.

Of the body, only the top of the skull, some teeth, some of the hair and both thigh bones seemed to remain. There was a break in one of the bones. As he surveyed the remains, an odd thought occurred: at last he was an archaeologist. He smiled tiredly, and spent the next while levelling off his excavation, so that the body lay in a neat rectangle.

He wiped his brow and eyed the great globe of the Sun as it crept down closer to the horizon. The head of the body lay pointing to the west. He looked back at the Stane. It seemed to lie west-east; exactly the same position as the body. Both seemed to point at the setting Sun.

Impulsively, he dropped the spade, ran up to the Stane and clambered on its back. Yes, it was true: the Stane and the body pointed at the Sun. He drew a line with his outstretched arm. No, not directly. They pointed just a little to the right of the Sun's present position. That would be just about where he estimated that the Sun would set.

Of course! Today was the Equinox!

He'd read that it was believed that the sun and moon were worshipped by the Ancient People back in the Neolithic and Bronze Ages. Surely, he reasoned, the position of the Sun on such a day, as well as on the Solstices, would be of crucial importance to the worshippers of these most ancient religions. Perhaps the Stane had been placed in its present position by these ancients as some marker of the midway point between the Solstices. Perhaps it had always lain thus, and was imbued with its own elemental magic. Perhaps indeed it was a marker to tap the great flow of Time in a place where one could be cast backwards or forwards on its Tide.

The Stane grew restless beneath him. For an instant a chorus of supplicatory voices swirled round him, then all was still. The disc of the Sun began to inflate. Its fires seemed to dim as it neared the horizon.

He slipped down from the Stane and stood once more by the grave. The Sun's orange glow tinged the Moss and suffused the body. Above it, a vapour danced like the play of evening mist. It rose and coiled, and briefly he imagined that he could glimpse a flicker of a smile on a grizzled visage. But there was something solid behind the mist. Someone standing, still as a tombstone at the head of the body. The murdered man for sure!

But as the mist evaporated, he saw that it was a soldier, pale, but with a wan smile on his face. A young officer. Where had he sprung from?

" Ye gave me a fricht," Tommy breathed in relief," ah never heard ye comin. Did Gerry send ye here?"

The soldier's smile spread, but he did not reply.

There was something familiar about him. Something recent. Something.......

The Photograph!

" Faither!"

Blubbering, Tommy rushed towards him, arms outstretched. The Apparition stepped back, but retained its smile. Confused, Tommy halted before it,

tears still trickling down his face.
" Faither, ye've come back tae see me, how did ye dae it?"
His Father eyed the Stane on the rise.
" Aye, ah understand, ye kent aboot aw this afore it happened. Ye saw it aw thae years ago. Ye kent that ye were gaun tae be killed, an ye kent that ye'd see me noo."
Love shone out from his Father's eyes. A love that transiently vanquished even Time.
" Faither," he shouted, as if his voice had to carry into the dark realms, " ah'm startin a job in a wee while, an when ah'm auld enough, ah'm gaun tae jine up. Yer auld Regiment, the H.L.I. Ah'm gaun tae be an officer juist like ye!"
A look of horror crossed the Spectre's face. His Father grew animated, and shook his head violently. Words spilled from his mouth, but no sound came. A far off shout echoed.
" Tommee!" That sounded like Gerry.
The Ghost jerked his head and fled from him into the great eye of the Sun, arms stretched out to him.
Madly, he clambered after it. " Faither, Faither!" he wailed hopelessly, but now there was nothing but Earth, Sky and Sun.
He sprawled over a tussock and tore at the earth, beside himself at the loss of his Father. He turned over and flailed at the sky in a frenzy for what seemed like an age.
The faint drum of footsteps approached.
" Calm doon Son, " a voice murmured gently. Through a tear haze, he could discern the figure of Wullie. He hauled himself up.
" Did ye see everything? Did ye see him Wullie?" he sobbed.
" Ah heard ye talkin tae yersel an shoutin efter somethin, but ah didnae see anythin." Wullie shook his head sadly.
" But ah saw ma Faither!"
" Aye, maybe ye did. Come on noo Son."
Wullie took him by the arm, and gently but insistently steered him back towards the grave.
" Wullie," he bubbled, " ah didnae have time tae tell him ah loved him!"
" Ah think he kens that," said Wullie softly.
Tommy mopped away his tears and together they gazed down at the remains of the murdered man.

" Aye, that's him right enough." Wullie beamed down at Tommy. " Ye've held yer end up. The Circle is Complete!"
Another shout, close at hand.
" Ower here Gerry, juist ower here!" yelled Tommy.
Wullie slunk away from his side.
" Are ye no steyin?"
" Naw, it'll no dae for me tae be seen here. Ah'll see ye again Son!"
Soundlessly, he padded off, and in a blink was gone. Tommy began to wonder if he had imagined his presence. He crested the rise by the Wutchstane. Not far off, Gerry and two important looking policemen approached. Behind them, two burly bobbies carried a stretcher between them.
He waved his arms. " Ower here!" he called.
As the policemen clustered round the body, Tommy stood by the Stane.
The Superintendent questioned Gerry closely, writing the details in his notebook. His Sergeant made sketches and took copious notes as the Constables shouted out details from the body.
Frequently, the Superintendent glanced significantly in Tommy's direction as an animated Gerry poured out his story. Finally, he snapped his notebook closed.
" C'mere Son," he beckoned Tommy down.
Obediently, Tommy complied. The policeman studied him intently.
" Superintendent Aitken, Bellshill Police," he announced grandly, " lucky ah wis visiting the Station at Newmains. And you are...." He consulted his notebook," Master Tommy Neill. Z'at right Son?"
Tommy nodded.
Superintendent Aitken tapped his pencil on the cover of his notebook. " Where d'ye stey Son?"
Tommy gave his address, and as the Superintendent jotted it down, he asked softly, " How did ye ken the man wis murdered Son? Ye said tae Mr. Rolink that he'd been murdered, and it wis you that brought Mr. Rolink here tae dig for peat, that's right, isn't it?"
" Aye," replied Tommy matter of factly.
He strode over to the body.
" Look, ah'll show yez!" He indicated the gashes in the cap and the shoe. " Ye can tell by thae cuts. He wis murdered aw richt, but ah think ye're ower late tae catch the wans that did it!"
The Superintendent smiled slowly, " Aye Son, he's been here for many a

lang year has this yin. Still, the hale matter's still tae be investigated: it's no for me tae say."
Gerry, now having recovered some of his composure, interjected, " Ah'll sweir on the Bible that this peat hasnae been disturbed for hunners o years!"
The Sergeant approached the trio, " Look at the claes, Sur. Juist the sort ye'd expect folk tae have worn in the aulden times."
Superintendent Aitken put his notebook away. He drew Tommy an old fashioned look and shook his head. " Are ye wantin tae be a detective when ye're aulder Son? Ye can have ma joab."
" Naw, no thanks Sir, ah'm gaun tae be a sodjer, juist like ma Da."
" Aw aye," smiled the Sergeant, " whit regiment is he in?"
Tommy smiled faintly, " He's deid Sir, he wis killt in the War."
" Sorry Son." The Sergeant blushed.
" Juist wan thing ," the Superintendent interrupted quickly; partly to save his Sergeant's embarrassment.
" Whit's that?"
" Why did ye say 'the wans that did it'. How d'ye ken there wis mair than wan murderer?"
Tommy shrugged," Juist a guess. It would probably take mair than wan person tae cairry the body."
" Ah Son, ye'll be wastit in the Army!" The Superintendent shook his head and tutted. " Anywey, this'll require a lot mair investigation. We'll telephone wan o thae fullahs at the Museum in Glasgow when we get back tae the Station."
" An Archaeologist?" asked Tommy.
" Aye, wan o thae......fullahs."
One of the Constables smirked. The Superintendent glared at him.
" Right, noo carefully transfer the corpse tae the stretcher. And ah want everythin in the right position juist as ye see it. Carefully ah said! But hurry it up, it'll be daurk shuin. Caunny Man!"
The Superintendent oversaw as the Sergeant and the two Constables set to work.
" Can ah go hame noo?" piped up Tommy, " ma Mammy'll be wonderin where ah've gaun tae."
" Aye, aw right. Ye'd best hurry hame; Mr Rolink can come up tae the Station for a few mair questions. Ye'll be hearin frae us though!"
Tommy nodded, but dallied until the remains were laid out on the stretcher.

" Right lads, let's git back tae the Station," instructed the Sergeant as the two Bobbies raised up the stretcher. He turned to his Superior,
" Anythin else Sur?"
" Naw, let's be on oor wey." He glanced at Tommy, " Awa hame Son, or yer Mammy'll be wonderin aboot ye."
" Aye, ah'm juist gaun."
" Ye've done a guid joab this day Son, but your part's aw feenished, ye can leave the rest o the business tae us. Cheerio, hurry up an get hame!"
Superintendent Aitken turned and made off, bringing up the rear of the doleful procession.
Still Tommy stood.
The man was right enough he thought. His role in the affair was over. He thought of the pathetic remains on the stretcher. Now, like the murdered man, he was free.
His eyes fastened on the Stane. It glowed like a beacon in Time, illuminated in the Sunset.

A Pillar of Fire rose in the Desert. The heat flayed his skin. A tank flared incandescently until it was consumed.
Two soldiers approached, deeply tanned and grumbling. Stumbling across the burning red sands, they bore a stretcher. A charred corpse lay on it, burned beyond recognition. Something glinted on the fused stump of its right hand.
The bearers crested a dune and were gone.
Now he was alone in the chill of the March evening.

The dirl of the pipes. A file of soldiers, led by a piper, marched jauntily by. There was Rab McKay, tall and strapping at the head of the file, pride shining in his eyes. There was Carrot Heid, spick and span in his tartan trews: there was Geordie Wilson. A few other familiar faces loomed among the eager young men.
Abruptly the march changed. A lament: ' The Flowers o the Forest'. In slow time, they marched into the last rays of the Sunset.

Tommy breathed deeply. The Moss was empty and silent. He'd had enough of these dreams. This was the last he determined.
Never again would he venture into this area of the Moss. He'd keep away

from things best left alone, then he'd be free of tricks of his imagination.
A deep growl reached his ears. He quivered, but almost immediately relaxed as he realised that it was the sound of a plane. The sound of reality. Across the western sky it bored, scarring the face of the Sun as it crept below the horizon. Even as it did so, the Furnace Doors in the Steelworks were flung open, enhancing the Sunset. As the sky flamed red somewhere a siren wailed. At last he turned for home.
He reflected on the vision of his Father. Whether real or imaginary, perhaps he'd found him, not lost him at all. At last he'd had a chance to greet over him. Anyway he'd make sure he'd be worthy of his Father's name. Aye, he'd make good and sure of that!

The Wutchstane dwindled behind him, pointing its arrow at the last red arch of the Sun. Its glow winked out and the World turned its face from the Light.